D0149284

BANK JOB

BANK JOB

STEVE BREWER

INTRIGUE PRESS | BOULDER

Book layout and design by CPG, www.corvuspublishinggroup.com

Library of Congress Cataloging-in-Publication Data

Brewer, Steve.
Bank job / by Steve Brewer.
p. cm.
ISBN-13: 978-1-890768-65-2
ISBN-10: 1-890768-65-0
1. Criminals--Fiction. 2. Bank robberies--Fiction. 3. California--Fiction. I.
Title.
PS3552.R42135B36 2005
813'.54--dc22
                                        2005020911

10 9 8 7 6 5 4 3 2 1

For Frank Zoretich and Kelly Brewer, the wielders of the red pens

1

Junior Daggett jolted out of a doze when the driver of the Trans Am, his brother Leon, broke the silence in the car: "Know what they call this in the newspapers? What we're doing?"

Roy Wade, a great lump of muscle in the shotgun seat, said, "What?"

"A 'crime spree,'" Leon said. "I always liked that. Sounds like a lot of fun, don't it?"

Roy snorted, as close to a laugh as you'd ever get out of him.

Junior yawned and stretched as best he could in the cramped back seat, thinking: Not much fun so far. Roaring around rural California in Leon's sleek black car, knocking over gas stations and convenience stores for small change. Swilling Buds and smoking Marlboros and whistling at passing women. Hell, as far as Junior could see, it was like a typical redneck Saturday night in Bakersfield.

"If the papers wrote about us, they'd call us 'criminals,' right?" Roy said to Leon. Neither paid any attention to Junior, who always felt he was eavesdropping on their conversations.

"Guess so," Leon said. "But we couldn't argue with that, could we? We *are* criminals. You commit crimes, you're a criminal. That's a fact."

"Never liked that term," Roy muttered. "Makes me think of 'convict.'"

"Well, hell, one thing does tend to lead to another. What would you suggest they call us? Rocket scientists? Rotarians?"

"Don't be a smartass."

Leon pushed his shaggy black hair back from his thick shelf of a brow and said, "Then tell me. What's the correct English term for what we are?"

Roy looked over at Leon, and Junior could see his full profile. The thrust-out jaw, the flattened nose, the narrow eyes, the side of his head shaved smooth over an undersized ear.

"Outlaws," Roy said.

Leon hooted and slapped the steering wheel with a meaty hand.

"I like *that*!" He glanced up at the rear-view mirror. "What do you think, Junior? Are we 'outlaws' or what?"

"If you say so." Junior shook his head, trying to clear the cobwebs from his brief nap.

Roy twisted his thick neck around so he could look over his shoulder at him. "You could show a little enthusiasm there, pup."

Junior took a deep breath, dreading what he was about to say. "I'd be more enthusiastic if we weren't lost."

"Lost?" Leon shouted. "Hell, we ain't lost. Roy knows exactly where we're going. Don't you, Roy?"

Roy squinted at Junior, his jaw set. He didn't like anyone questioning him. He'd said earlier that he knew the area, but Junior didn't see how that was possible. They were a long way from Bakersfield, and he was sure Roy had never traveled this far north. They'd been driving for hours, ever since their lunch in a town called Red Bluff came to an abrupt halt.

Even *lunch* couldn't go smoothly when Roy Wade was around. Roy's burger had been overcooked, and he made a lot of noise about how it looked like a "fuckin' hockey puck," disturbing the few other diners in the roadside eatery. Their scrawny old waitress finally had enough of him and called for the owner, who came out from the kitchen in his filthy apron, ready to give Roy some shit. The owner must've been in his fifties, but he looked stout and damned unhappy at the uproar. He barely got three words out of his mouth before Roy flashed to his feet and rapid-punched him, sending blood and teeth flying across the cafe. The violence was so sudden and frightening, it made Junior spill his Coke in his lap. His jeans were still sticky.

They'd scooted out of there before anybody could call the cops, so Junior hadn't finished eating. Now, his stomach growled, as if in answer to Roy's glare.

"You in charge now, Junior?" Roy said. "You gonna tell us where to go?"

"I didn't say that—"

"Then shut the hell up."

"Come on, Roy," Leon said. "Take it easy."

"Fuck that. Your brother's done nothing but complain since we started on this trip. I told you not to bring him."

"Aw, he didn't mean nothin'."

"Then he better learn to keep his mouth shut. You hear me, boy? If you don't *mean* nothin', then you don't *say* nothin'. Got it?"

Junior nodded. He looked out the window at the endless pine trees whizzing past, waiting for Roy to turn away, to forget about him.

He was pretty sure they were lost. They'd roared out of Red Bluff on some little piss-ant highway, driving straight into the blinding afternoon sun, bypassing Interstate 5, which seemed the smarter way to travel. Straight shot up the Central Valley, lots of other cars to use for cover. Even Leon's thirty-year-old Pontiac with its gold-tone rims and its firebird painted on the hood stood a chance of blending in on I-5. But no, Leon had to take Roy's word that he knew the territory. Leon always listened to him over Junior, who was stuck for life with the role of snot-nosed little brother.

Roy was terminally stupid, but he projected absolute certainty about absolutely everything. Leon often fell for such confidence. Or maybe it was just easier not to argue with stubborn Roy. Leon probably figured it was better to be lost than to tangle with his bad-tempered partner. But Junior didn't like not knowing where they were.

Hell, they didn't even have a map. Junior had suggested picking one up a week ago, when they left Bakersfield, but that had been met with more snarling derision. Guess "outlaws" did everything by dead reckoning. Probably why so many end up behind bars.

If it had been up to Junior, they would've headed west, gone over to the coast to check out sprawling Los Angeles, see the ocean, go to fucking Disneyland. He'd lived in the Golden State all his life, but it wasn't the place most folks pictured when they heard "California." Junior's California was on the outskirts of town, a land of blistering heat and junkyards and vacant lots and tumbleweeds. Worlds away from Hollywood and Rodeo Drive and sandy beaches and Pacific sunsets. He'd like to visit L. A., see what all the fuss was about.

But where did Leon take them? North. Zig-zagging up the flat Central Valley, through stubbled cropland and dusty little towns. Mile after mile of orderly orchards and flooded rice paddies and smelly dairies, all of which made Bakersfield look like a freaking paradise.

The land had begun to roll around Red Bluff—hills and creeks and canyons breaking up the flat monotony of the agricultural valley. As they traveled northwest, the hills grew into mountains and the landscape surrendered to wild forests. They'd gone through a few little towns, places with names like Platina and Wildwood, Peanut and Hayfork, but Leon hadn't stopped in any of them. Hell, nothing in those towns to stop *for*. Now there was nothing but forest in every direction, trees climbing up hillsides and trees dipping down canyons and trees reaching out from the shoulders of the narrow, twisting highway. For all Junior could tell, they might be in Oregon.

Some trees still bore the reds and golds of autumn, though it was nearly Thanksgiving, but most were wispy pines and other evergreens that made the whole landscape look fuzzy. A light rain slicked the pavement and sprinkled the windows with diamonds in the dying light.

Junior didn't like it up here. He preferred flatlands and bare desert, places where a man could see for miles. Up here, he kept getting the itchy feeling that speed traps lurked around every highway curve, that cops could materialize out of the mist at any second and put a harsh end to this "crime spree."

He twisted on the tiny seat, trying to get more comfortable. At twenty-three, he was five years younger and eighty pounds lighter than either of the bruisers up front, and there never was any question who'd ride in back. He wished they would hit another town, a rest area, something, so they'd have a reason to stop and stretch their legs.

They passed a couple of houses tucked among the trees, giving Junior hope of civilization up ahead. Then the Trans Am crested a hill and a green sign glowed in the headlights: "Douglas City, Junction U. S. 299, 1 mile," it said. "Redding. Eureka."

Roy smirked. "See there, you little shit? I told you we wasn't lost. We'll turn east up here, go to Redding. That's a pretty big town, as I recall. We can get some dinner, find a motel."

For Junior, this place Redding couldn't come soon enough. Get out of the car, get some fresh air, take a piss, eat some supper. His stomach growled again.

Scattered buildings popped up alongside the highway, but Leon reached the junction without stopping anywhere. Just turned onto the wider highway and let the engine unwind. Another sign: "Redding—42 miles." Junior stifled a moan.

Within minutes, they were surrounded again by steep hills

and shadowy forests. Leon tried to pick up the pace, but they kept getting caught behind gear-grinding logging trucks and Winnebagos poking up the hills.

Darkness fell as the miles crawled past. Leon kept up a steady stream of patter, talking about women he'd screwed and parties he'd enjoyed and adventures he'd shared with Roy. Junior knew his long-winded brother was trying to lighten the mood in the car, but it didn't seem to be working. Roy silently slugged beer and smoked one cigarette after another, still stewing.

The car climbed a long hill, and signs said, "Whiskeytown Lake," but Junior couldn't see any water. Just a tree-studded bluff that dropped away to darkness. A few lights around what looked like a visitors' center, locked up for the night.

They covered a couple more miles, saw more lights up ahead. A road sign flashed past that said "Shasta." Leon slowed the car. The little town was old, some of its half-dozen commercial buildings nothing more than empty brick shells. Lights glowed outside a store and some kind of museum, both with porches and squared-off false fronts, like buildings in a Western. Both looked buttoned-up tight for the night.

Shasta was only a few blocks long, and neon glowed at the far end. Roy said, "Look. Ain't that a liquor store? We need more beer."

Junior sighed. Redding couldn't be more than another six or seven miles up ahead. Why stop now?

Leon hit the brakes and steered the Trans Am into the muddy lot. The store had none of the charm of the historic buildings. Just a concrete cube with a flickering neon sign on top that said: "Shasta Liquors." The front windows were dirty and smudged, letting only feeble yellow light through iron grillework.

"Looks like it's still open," Leon said.

He parked in the darkest spot beside the building. He and Roy exchanged a look, their faces illuminated by the glow from the dashboard.

The light glinted on the shaved sides of Roy's head. The black stripe of his slicked-back Mohawk made him look like his head had been cleaved. Leon was a shadow, his curly black hair and beard absorbing all light, his shovel of a brow burying his eyes in darkness.

Roy popped open the glove compartment and retrieved his .38-caliber Smith & Wesson. The snubnose revolver gleamed in the dash light. Junior thinking, here we go again.

Roy said, "Why don't we let the pup pull this one?"

Leon glanced back at Junior, then said, "I don't know, Roy. Maybe I oughta do it."

"It's time Junior started pulling his weight. He's done nothing but pout since we started this trip."

Leon tilted the rearview mirror, trying to see Junior's face. "How about it, little brother? You ready for the big time?"

Junior tried to come up with some reason he couldn't knock over the store, something that wouldn't shame him forever in their eyes. His brain ticked slowly, and he heard himself say, "Sure."

"That a boy," Roy said. "You can use my gun."

He tilted the barrel toward the roof of the car, popped open the cylinder, and shook the bullets into a cupped hand. "But you don't want it loaded. Might shoot your dick off by accident."

Leon said, "You want to send the boy into that store with an empty gun?"

"All he's gotta do is flash it. They'll hand over the dough and he's out of there."

"I don't know, Roy. Some of these assholes keep heat under the counter."

"He'll be in and out so quick, they won't have a chance. Ain't that right?"

Junior sputtered, "If you say so."

Roy handed him the pistol. "Besides, if the gun's not loaded, then it ain't a felony. We get caught, you won't have to do much time."

Junior was pretty sure *that* was bullshit. Armed robbery was armed robbery, bullets or no. But he didn't say so. Once Roy Wade got an idea in his head, there was no arguing with him. Like talking to a rock.

Roy got out of the car and stretched his bulging arms up over his shoulders, working out the kinks, while Junior climbed out of the back seat. It was still sprinkling, and cold raindrops hit Junior's head. One sneaked inside his collar, making him shiver.

"Do good, little brother," Leon said. "Make me proud."

Junior walked around the rear of the car on shaky legs, stuffing the heavy gun in his belt, under his chambray shirt. He straightened his shoulders and clenched his hands into fists to keep them from trembling. The damp chill made him wish he hadn't left his jacket in the car.

Roy said behind him, "And get a case of Bud."

Junior had known all along they'd expect him to take a turn. Roy had teased him all week about how he'd never done any time, never shown his "manhood" as a felon. He'd committed plenty of misdemeanors: Smoked a lot of grass, and dealt a little now and then. Often gone joy-riding in hot cars with his brother or stood watch while Leon lifted hubcaps. But sticking up a liquor store? Never anything close.

He took a deep breath and pushed through the store's heavy glass door. A bell jangled and he nearly jumped out of his skin.

The store looked like every other hooch shop in the world, if a little dirtier than most. Cheap paneling on the walls and a scuffed green concrete floor, gray showing through where dollies and crates had chipped away the paint over the years. An island of cheap rotgut stood in sawed-off boxes in the center of the room. A beer cooler way in the back. Wine bottles on rough wooden shelves along one wall. More shelves behind the counter to keep the good stuff out of reach. Bounced checks and other papers covered the countertop in a mess of Scotch tape, surrounding an antique cash register.

A chunky old woman stood behind the counter, a yellow Schlitz sign glowing above her head like a hard-luck halo. Her gray hair was chopped short, and she wore a polyester sack of a blouse decorated with pink flamingos. She glared at Junior through thick glasses, but he felt encouraged that the clerk was a woman. Might be easier to bluff.

He wrenched the pistol from his waistband, wincing as the gunsight snagged a painful scratch up his belly, and pointed it at the woman's wrinkled face.

"Hands up!" he shouted, his voice sounding squeaky and unfamiliar.

The clerk's face twisted into a scowling prune. Her flabby arms stayed by her sides.

"I said put your hands in the air!" he squeaked. "This is a stickin' fuck-up!"

As soon as the words were out of his mouth, Junior wished he could suck them back in. Eat them.

The old woman snorted. Her face melted into a grandma smile and her eyes glinted behind the glasses. Something about her made Junior think of Halloween. The witch who smiles sweetly while she hands out the poisoned candy.

She cocked her head and her blue eyes flicked upward. Junior glanced up to see where she was looking.

A small television hung from the ceiling, dusty and black. An image flickered on the thirteen-inch screen, and he looked right into his own wide eyes. Surveillance video. Junior caught in living color. Aw, shit.

The clerk moved on the screen. No, wait a second, it wasn't her. This woman looked like the clerk, but her gray hair was stringy and long, down to her shoulders. She was *behind* Junior, closing fast. She carried a fifth of whiskey by the neck. Cocked back over her shoulder like a club.

He wheeled, just in time to catch the swinging bottle squarely on the forehead. It crashed over his face, sounded like a car wreck inside his head. He saw a flash of white light. Pain split his face. Whiskey stung his eyes.

"Aaaaugh!" He staggered backward. Could barely make out anything through his marinated eyeballs, just shapes and light. He blinked and shook his head, got back just enough vision to see the long-haired woman snatch up another bottle and swing it.

Crash against the side of his head, just above the ear. Junior stumbled backward until his hips hit the counter. Then another bottle smashed over his head from behind.

Booze and blood blinded him. He swung the empty gun around, wildly waving his other hand, hacking his way through the liquor fumes, trying to keep the harpies off him.

"You son of a bitch!" one screamed.

Junior lurched toward the door, knocking a row of bottles off the center display. The bottles exploded on the concrete floor. He stumbled out the door, the bell jangling merrily over his head.

Cold dark outside, the women still shrieking somewhere behind him. Junior blindly veered to his left, toward the car. Big hands grabbed him and roughly dragged him along. Snatched the gun from his hand. Threw him into the back seat.

The Trans Am roared and mud thudded inside the fender wells. The car bucked up onto the blacktop and Leon floored it, thundering curses while he drove.

Junior brushed at his eyes, his breath coming in gasping whimpers. His hands and face and neck were sticky with blood. His crotch was hot with urine. His brain was filling with gray lint.

He felt Roy's hands on him again, pulling him upright, wiping at his face. Lights flashed in Junior's head and he sucked air, trying to remain conscious against the waves of pain.

Roy said flatly, "You forgot the fuckin' beer."

2

Leon Daggett gripped the leather-wrapped steering wheel in both hands, squeezing so hard that the thick muscles in his tattooed forearms stood at attention. He slalomed the Trans Am through a curve, tires slipping on the wet asphalt, headlight beams slicing through the misty night.

"How bad's he hurt?" he shouted over the roaring engine.

"Shit, I can't tell," said Roy, who was twisted around, up on his knees in the bucket seat, his hands busy with Junior. "Too much fuckin' blood."

Junior bawled and gasped, his breath coming in fits and shudders. The air in the car stank of blood and whiskey and piss and fear.

An unwelcome thought flitted through Leon's head: Damn, I just had the seats reupholstered. Junior's bleeding all over my rich Corinthian leather.

He stomped the accelerator and the car bounded up a hill like a panther. Then he was forced to hit the brakes as the road snaked to the left, another goddamned curve.

"Cops'll be all over in a minute," Roy said. "Get off this fuckin' highway."

"And go where?" Leon bellowed. "There's nothing out here but goddamn trees!"

Junior howled at Roy's ministrations, making Leon ever more frantic. He had to do something. They were within a few miles of Redding. They could find a doctor, an emergency room.

"Little brother needs medical attention!"

"Fuck that," Roy said. "We show up at a hospital, and we're all going straight to jail."

"He'll bleed to death! I'll never hear the end of it from Mama."

Another curve, back the other way. Leon slowed, then gunned the car into a straightaway. The Trans Am gobbled up the glowing yellow dashes in the middle of the wet highway.

"I need light," Roy said.

"Can't turn on the light. I can't see the road now."

"Pull over somewhere."

"There's nothing but woods."

"Just fuckin' pull over."

Leon's eyes scanned the shoulders of the highway. Trees marched in tight formation to the edge of the road on one side. On the other, the narrow shoulder sloped down into the dark, looked like a canyon, could be a mile deep for all he could tell. A few lights flickered high on the hilltops, but if there were houses up there, he couldn't see any way to reach them.

"Shit, shit, shit!"

"Quit hollering and stop the car."

Junior huffed and sobbed. Leon couldn't stand it, hearing his brother hurt so.

Then he saw a light up ahead, on the right, flickering through trees near the edge of the highway. Leon stood on the brakes, and the back end fishtailed, but he got the car under control, wrestled it to a halt. The headlight beams caught the shiny edge of a steel culvert. A driveway. Leon hooked a right, the car bouncing through mudholes.

Pine trees grew tight on either side of the narrow driveway.

The needles of their reaching limbs paintbrushed the sides of the car. The driveway ended fifty feet from the road at a pitched-roof cabin, the porch light on, welcoming them.

"Turn on the inside light," Roy said tightly.

"Fuck that. I'm getting some help."

"Leon—"

But Leon was out of the car, his pistol in his hand. His cowboy boots clumped up flagstone steps onto the wide wooden porch. The cabin was crafted of peeled logs, varnished the color of honey. Two large windows were cut into the thick walls, either side of the front door, but they were covered by thick curtains. The wooden door had a tiny window set into it, light shining through. Leon hammered the door with his fist.

He spied movement through the little window. Silver hair, a flash of red.

A woman swung open the door. She was probably seventy, and her shoulder-length hair was parted in the middle, framing a lined face and shiny black eyes. She looked to Leon like an Indian or maybe a Mexican, an effect heightened by the red tunic she wore, which had black embroidery zig-zagging around the neckline. She smiled, and her teeth looked dazzlingly white against her coppery skin.

"Yes?"

Leon was a good foot taller than the woman and he could see over her head. The whole front of the cabin was a large living room lined with bookcases. Hardwood floors and oval rugs and overstuffed furniture. At the far end, an archway opened into a kitchen; Leon could see cabinets beyond and a wooden table and chairs.

A wiry, straight-backed old man with a mane of thick white hair appeared in the archway. Average height and trimly built, with a strong chin and oversized hands. Dressed in khakis and a plaid flannel shirt. The man stayed where he was, his cottony eyebrows raised in question.

"We need help," Leon said to the woman.

A look of concern immediately rose on her face. She leaned to one side, trying to see around him to where Junior caterwauled in the car. Her eyes dipped and she spotted the pistol Leon held by his hip, pointed her way.

She gasped and took a single step back, ready to run, then caught herself and froze. She looked up at him, her eyes wide with fear.

"Certainly," she said, a tremor in her voice. "Won't you come in?"

"Damned right I will."

3

Vince Carson's heart leaped when he saw the gun, but he had no time to react. The intruder shoved his way past Maria and raised his hand, pointed the black semi-automatic.

"Just be still, dad," he growled.

The bearded man was nearly as tall as the doorway and his shoulders were nearly as wide. Looked to be in his late twenties, hairy and unkempt. Dirty blue jeans tight on muscular legs, sun-baked cowboy boots, a black "Lynyrd Skynyrd" T-shirt cut off raggedly at the shoulders to expose slabs of arm. Tattoo of a coiling green dragon on his left forearm, a murky hula dancer on the right. A web inked around the right elbow with a little spider dangling off one side, appearing to menace the island girl. The man's eyes were wild under a caveman brow.

He grasped Maria's shoulder, his fingernails dirty against her red blouse. Vince bristled at the sight of that hand on his wife, but he tried to keep the feelings off his face. He could feel his heart pounding, the adrenaline coursing through his body, his muscles twitching with the desire to stop this before it got any worse.

Maria's dark eyes were wide and wet with sudden tears. Her mouth gaped. Her gaze flitted from Vince to the bearded man and back again, searching, trying to make sense of it all.

The intruder shouted back over his shoulder. "Bring him in,

Roy!" He stepped out of the doorway, but kept his hand on Maria's shoulder and the pistol pointed at Vince.

Beyond him, an old black Pontiac was parked at the end of the flagstone walkway that stepped down from the porch. A hard-looking muscle boy, even more pumped-up than the tattooed guy, half-carried a skinny kid up the steps. The kid's face was awash in blood, and his blue shirt was soaked with red halfway down his chest. His eyes were squinched shut and his mouth was a ragged hole.

"*Dios mio*," said Maria, wiping at her eyes. "What happened to this child?"

She twisted out of the tall man's grasp and hurried toward the injured boy.

Vince shook his head. Maria. Always the nurse.

She went onto the porch and got hold of the kid from the other side, helped the muscle boy edge him through the door. Blood dripped on the floor.

Vince turned to the kitchen and grasped a wooden chair. The man with the gun yelled, "Hey!" But Vince came back through the archway with the straight-backed chair before he could decide to shoot.

He carried the chair across the living room, kicked a small rug out of the way and set the chair on bare hardwood near the door so they could sit the kid on it. He smelled like a bathroom in a saloon—urine and whiskey and blood.

"I need the first-aid kit," Maria said. Her quick eyes ran over the wounded man, sizing up the injuries. "And some towels."

Vince returned to the kitchen, this time with the bearded one right on his heels.

Doors opened off the kitchen on either side—bedroom and bathroom to the left, a laundry room/pantry tucked in the corner to the right, past the sink and fridge. Vince went into the pantry, the big man filling the door behind him, and bent over to look through the supplies on the shelves.

The man jabbed the gun barrel in Vince's back, and said, "Careful, dad."

Instant resentment flooded through Vince, but he kept his hands still and his voice calm. "You want bandages or you want that kid to bleed to death?"

"Just don't try anything."

Vince lifted a plastic tackle box off a shelf and straightened up. Turned to face the intruder.

The bearded man was six inches taller, but Vince met his eyes and they stared at each other. Vince could feel the gun against his chest, but he didn't look down at the pistol, didn't break the eye-lock.

The larger man finally blinked. He nudged Vince with the gun and said, "Hurry up."

Vince took a stack of neatly folded dishtowels off another shelf. He carried it all to Maria, not hurrying.

The other bruiser was pushing bullets into the chambers of a revolver. His hands were covered in the wounded man's blood. He was about Vince's height, but twice as wide. He wore a gray sweatshirt with short sleeves that were stretched tight by bulging biceps. The sides and back of his head were shaved and tanned. The dark strip of hair on top was short and slicked straight back. The hairstyle was like a billboard saying, "Moron." But Vince recognized something in the hard glitter of the man's eyes and amended the assessment: "Dangerous moron."

Vince opened the tackle box, which contained medical supplies neatly arranged in its inner shelves, and held it for Maria, who used a towel to gently mop the blood away from the young man's eyes and forehead.

The kid's scalp was covered in oozing slashes. Pieces of what looked like bloody glass stuck up from his short black hair.

"The hell happened to you?" Vince asked.

"They—" the kid began, then took a deep, shuddering breath. "They broke bottles over my head."

"These guys?"

"Nooo," the kid sobbed. "Those women."

Vince couldn't make any sense of that. At Maria's instructions, he pulled over a small table and set the first-aid kit on it, within her reach. Then he went to the kitchen for a glass of water and more towels. The bearded man stayed right with him, keeping the gun trained on him.

"Why don't you put those pistols away before somebody else gets hurt?"

"Fuck you," the man said. "Just help her out. She seems to know what she's doing."

"She should," Vince said as he returned to the living room. "She's a nurse."

Once they were again working on Junior, the bearded man said, "I got 'em covered, Roy. Go wash your hands."

The one with the stupid haircut held his red hands out before him, looking them over like he was surprised to discover they were sticky with blood. He stuck the revolver in his belt and sauntered toward the kitchen. Vince heard him slamming doors back there. Then he heard water running in the kitchen.

Maria shook two white pills into the palm of her hand from a brown prescription bottle.

"Open your mouth," she told the whimpering kid. She put the pills on his tongue, then had him drink water to wash them down.

"Codeine," she said. "They'll help block some of the hurt."

The kid nodded and blinked his teary eyes. He glanced around the room, finally able to see his surroundings.

"Where am I?" he managed. "Who are you?"

"My name's Maria and this is my husband, Vince. You're in our living room." Maria's voice was even and soft, no trace of the panic she'd shown a few moments before. She'd slipped into medical mode, composed and efficient. Vince had seen her like this before.

The kid looked glassy-eyed, and Vince wasn't sure he'd heard anything she said. She gently swabbed at his head with a fresh towel and Vince noticed that, despite the outward calm, her hands were trembling.

"He needs stitches," she said. "And we need to get the glass out of these wounds."

"Leon?" the kid said. "I'm scared."

"Take it easy, Junior. This lady here's a nurse. She'll fix you up."

"A *retired* nurse," Maria said. "This child needs more than I can offer him. He should go to a hospital."

"Not gonna happen," Leon blurted.

Roy came back from the kitchen, his sneakers thudding on the hardwood floor, water dripping off his hands.

"I checked out back," he said. "There's a garage out there. One car, but nobody else around."

Leon said, "Good. We might need that car later."

Vince didn't like the sound of that.

Roy pulled the revolver from the waistband of his black jeans and used it to wave Vince away from Maria and the kid.

"Go sit over there," he said, gesturing toward an old leather sofa. "Keep your hands where I can see 'em."

"I already told your friend," Vince said. "You don't need the guns. Maria will help the kid. Hell, we couldn't stop her if we tried."

Maria rolled her eyes, but her hands kept busy with Junior.

"Just sit the fuck down."

Vince did as he was told, taking his time, thoughts flitting through his head. Once he was on the sofa, his hands on his knees, he said, "You on the run from the law?"

Roy scowled and pointed his gun at Vince's face. "What makes you say that, old man?"

"Your friend said you can't go to the hospital. You gamble on busting into somebody's house to get the kid fixed up. Don't sound like regular citizens to me."

Roy cocked an eyebrow. "So you're a smart guy—"

"Roy!" Leon barked. "Go check the car. Throw one of these towels in the back seat to soak up that blood. And bring in Junior's bag. He'll need fresh clothes."

Roy held his eyes on Vince for a moment, oozing menace, then he looked over as Leon tossed him the car keys. He caught them and abruptly turned away, grabbing up a blue towel from the stack by Maria on his way to the door. He looked back at the open door and pointed the gun at Vince. Mouthed, "Pow." Then he went out into the night.

A look of exasperation passed over Leon's face. He said, "Don't mess with Roy, dad. He's got a temper."

Vince thinking: So do I. The initial shock was gone now, and he felt anger welling up within him. It was difficult to keep himself under control. These mutts come busting into his house, flashing their pieces, pushing people around—

Junior howled. Maria stood over him, oversized tweezers in her hand, holding up a shark's fin of bloody glass.

"One down," she said. "Two more to go."

Junior sat with his hands tight between his knees. Watched Maria with wet puppy eyes.

"It hurts."

"I know. But this glass has got to come out. Just sit still. We'll have you fixed up in a minute."

"You can stop the bleeding?" Leon asked.

"I think so. He'll need a few stitches. But I can do that, too."

Junior whimpered.

"Where did this happen?" she asked.

"Liquor store up the road," Leon said. "Junior went in there and, uh, I guess there was some kind of disagreement."

"They broke bottles over my head," Junior hiccuped. "A bunch of 'em."

"*Híjola*. You'll be lucky if you don't have a concussion."

Maria fished a penlight out of the first-aid kit and shined it in the kid's bloodshot eyes, back and forth, checking his pupils.

Vince still was thinking about the "disagreement" at the liquor store. He knew that store; it was the closest place to the cabin where he could buy ice. He could picture those two sisters breaking bottles on Junior's cranium, but not over any "disagreement."

"Junior tried to stick them up?" he asked.

Leon's eyes widened. The gun jerked in his hand, and Vince told himself to stop surprising the big galoot. These boys were amateurs, and that made them prone to mistakes. Vince needed them to relax. He needed to show them they were safe here. He tried to think of something to say, something to put them at ease.

Leon had a wary look on his Cro-Magnon face. "You're pretty quick, aren't you, dad?"

Vince shrugged, thinking: Not quick enough. I need some way out of this mess.

"You a cop?"

A bark of nervous laughter escaped Maria's lips before she caught herself. She turned her back to Leon, put the light back in the kit, and picked up the bloody tweezers again. Vince felt himself grinning.

Leon's face clouded with suspicion. "What's so funny?"

"I'm not a cop," Vince said. "Look at me. I'm seventy-two years old. I've been retired for years."

A car door slammed outside and Roy thumped back up onto the porch. Leon didn't take his eyes off Vince.

"What did you do before you *retired*?"

Over her shoulder, Maria gave Vince a cautioning look. He smiled her off.

"I was a bank robber."

Leon's mouth gaped, then spread into a wide grin.

"No shit?"

4

Shasta County Sheriff's Deputy Debra Kemp stepped carefully around the shattered glass, the spattered blood, the puddles of reeking booze on the floor at Shasta Liquors. The Bingham sisters waited for her behind the counter, big smiles on their round faces despite the mess all around them. Both wore thick eyeglasses and loud blouses. One said, "Well, well, if it's not Deputy Debby."

"Debra," she corrected automatically. God, she hated that nickname.

She hitched at her black webbed-leather belt, weighted down with a radio and handcuffs and extra magazines and her collapsible baton and her holstered Glock. No danger she'd lose the belt, not with her wide hips, but she found herself constantly adjusting her gear, trying to keep the belt from chafing.

A strand of dark hair had come loose from her ponytail. It fell down over her eye and she huffed it out of the way before she said, "What the heck happened here? Who's been bleeding?"

"About time you got here," one sister said.

"If we waited for you people to show up, we'd be dead by now," said the other.

"Or out of business."

Always the first thing deputies heard: The response time's too slow. Five night-shift deputies patrolling the entire mountainous expanse of Shasta County—nearly 4,000 square miles—but every-one expected a deputy to be just around the corner. Debra pushed ninety at times on the way here, but it still took twenty minutes to travel from way to hell and gone, over in Happy Valley, where she'd been settling a very *un*happy domestic dispute.

"Dispatch said the robber's long-gone," she said. "That he didn't even take anything. What's the hurry?"

"He could've come back," one sister said.

They laughed, and the other said, "Though I don't think that boy will bother anybody else for a while."

Debra sighed. She took her notebook out of the hip pocket of her olive-drab pants and a pen from the pocket of her khaki shirt.

"Why don't we start at the beginning?"

"We can do better than that," said the short-haired sister. Debra believed her name was Coral, but she wasn't certain. She'd always gotten the two sisters mixed up. Coral and Pearl, named by a seagoing father, though they were both stranded 150 miles from the Pacific. "We can show it to you on TV. Ain't that right, Pearl?"

Pearl pushed her long hair back out of her face, then pointed at the dusty video monitor suspended from the ceiling.

"We got the whole thing on tape," she said. "We've been watching it over and over, waiting for you."

"It's pretty good," Coral crowed. "Maybe we'll send it to one of those TV programs, the ones that show the funniest home videos."

Debra rolled her eyes. "It's evidence."

"We'll make a copy," Pearl said. "Here. Watch."

She pushed a button on a black console on the shelf behind her. The TV's dark screen illuminated and Debra tilted her head back to watch the flickering image.

Coral stood behind the counter on the video, the store other-wise empty. A slender man entered. Early twenties, about five-ten, 150 pounds, short black hair, wearing jeans and sneakers and a loose blue shirt. He made his way to the counter, reached under the shirt and came up with a revolver, pointed it at Coral.

"Too bad we don't have sound," Coral said. "You know what he said?"

The young man gestured jerkily with the gun.

"He said, 'This is a stickin' fuck-up.'" The old women cackled loud and long.

Debra smiled, but she didn't take her eyes off the video.

The camera was mounted on the ceiling and the angle was bad, but she was pretty sure she'd never seen the perp before. She'd grown up in Shasta County, probably knew half the residents on sight. And, having spent four years working in the county jail in downtown Redding before she finally made it to patrol six months ago, she recognized virtually every local who'd had recent trouble with the law.

Then Pearl appeared on the video, sneaking up behind the robber, a bottle of whiskey held high. The robber looked up, right at the camera, then wheeled just as she smashed the bottle over his head.

"Oh, my God," Debra said. No wonder there was blood all over the floor.

On the screen, Pearl snatched up another bottle. Cracked that one against his head, too. Behind him, Coral got into the act, grabbing a bottle off a shelf and bashing him with it.

He staggered away, and Pearl just missed as she swung another bottle at his head. Then he was out the door, Pearl chasing after him, her gray hair streaming behind, her lips flapping. She stopped when she reached the door, though, didn't pursue him out into the night. Which, Debra thought, was just as well. No telling who else might've been out there.

"A car took off a few seconds later," Pearl said. "It was parked around the corner of the building, waiting on him."

"Could you identify the make?"

"Hell, I don't know anything about cars."

Debra sighed.

Pearl brightened. "I tell you what it looked like, though. That black car Burt Reynolds drove in that old movie."

That narrowed it down to a few dozen.

"What was that movie called?" Pearl asked her sister. "The one where Burt wore that cowboy hat, talked on the CB all the time."

Smokey and the Bandit. Coral was smug, knowing the answer to the trivia question.

"Yeah, that one," Pearl said. "You're probably too young to remember it."

Debra, who'd celebrated her twenty-eighth birthday a few weeks earlier, thought: That movie came out before I was born. But she said, "I've seen it on TV. Think he drove a Trans Am."

The women shrugged. Both still grinning, gloating over how they'd defeated the criminal element, using the weapons at hand.

"If that *had* been Burt Reynolds trying to rob us," Coral said. "We wouldn't have hit him with those bottles."

"Bet your ass on that," Pearl agreed. "Hell, I'd give Burt *all* the money. And pour him a drink, too."

They snickered.

"Dream on, girls," Debra said, briefly wondering whether the two plump women had been "big-boned" like her when they were younger, and if that's why neither had ever married. She shook her head to clear those thoughts. Don't go *there.*

"Which way was the car headed?"

"Toward Redding," Pearl said.

That didn't help much. If they were local, the robbers could've been going home. If they were out-of-towners, they could still hide in the city, or head for a hospital, or go straight through to I-5 and be gone.

Debra looked around the store, rerunning in her mind how the attempted robbery had gone down. She needed to collect some of the blood off the floor for the crime lab. Check for tire tracks outside. Maybe check for fingerprints, though it looked on the video as if the robber hadn't touched anything but the door handle, which would yield the prints of half the drunks in the county. She imagined what her superior, Lieutenant Frank Jones, would say if she asked for the full lab treatment for an *attempted* robbery. She'd come across as an overzealous rookie. Again.

"You didn't recognize that boy?" she asked.

"Never seen him before," Coral said.

Pearl said, "He ought to be easy to spot now, though. Just look for somebody with glass in his head."

"And he'll smell like whiskey," Coral added.

The whole store smelled like booze. The fumes made Debra feel light-headed. Maybe, she thought, that's what's wrong with these sisters. High on booze vapors and adrenaline.

"Guess we're heroes, huh?" Coral said. "Think we ought to call the TV stations?"

Debra shook her head, thinking: Yeah, that's what we need added to the mix.

She wished the old women would stop distracting her with their yammering. She was trying to think. Something on the video was bothering her: When Pearl and Coral started attacking him with those bottles, why didn't the robber *shoot* them?

"Hey," Pearl said. "Maybe there's a price on that boy's head. We could get a *re*-ward!"

Maybe, Debra thought, I should shoot them myself.

5

Vince knew he'd taken a risk, mentioning his criminal past to these hoodlums. They might take it as a challenge, a reason to test him. He was gambling they'd see it the other way—as common ground—and it would help everybody relax.

He'd never bought into the whole brotherhood-of-thieves bullshit himself. He worked solo most of his long career, only taking on partners when there was absolutely no other way to pull a heist. Even then, he never turned his back on them, tried to never put himself in a position where they could rip him off or rat him out. Vince knew there was damned little honor among regular folks—hard-working, church-going citizens. Which meant there was *none* among thieves, no matter how much they might try to persuade you otherwise.

Vince spent half his adult life behind bars, and he hadn't met a con yet who wouldn't sell you out. Junior didn't look like he'd done any time—skinny wimp like him would've never made it out of stir alive. But the other two had prison-yard eyes and the overdeveloped muscles that came from plenty of empty time filled with weight-lifting.

Vince didn't trust them. Didn't want to be their pal. Didn't want anything from them except to escape the current situation with no harm coming to Maria. But he could play the experienced old pro, if that's what it took to get these losers to stop pointing those pistols.

It worked, too. The hairy one, Leon, tucked his gun into his belt and pulled up a chair, ready to jaw. But Roy, who looked like a fucking psycho, stayed on red alert, scowling at Vince and casting anxious glances out the open front door.

Maria ignored them, busy working on the injured kid. Junior sat very still while she worked with needle and thread, stitching shut the worst of the gashes. He made little mewling noises in his throat, but his trusting eyes never left her face.

"How many bank jobs you pull?" Leon asked. An eager light burned in his dark eyes.

"Ninety-three," Vince answered matter-of-factly.

"Goddamn! That's what I call a long career."

Vince nodded. "Beats working for a living."

"Ain't that the truth. Make a lot of big hauls?"

"A few. Biggest one was a job I pulled with a couple of other guys in Phoenix in 1975. Had an inside man at a Wells Fargo branch. Hijacked an armored car, put on the guards' uniforms, walked right into the bank and emptied the vault."

"And used the Wells Fargo truck to make your getaway?"

"That's right."

"You hear that, Roy? Now *that's* a heist! No penny-ante bullshit for this guy."

Vince thought Leon might be making fun of him, but he kept his face impassive. These jerks could laugh all they want, as long as he and Maria got out of this thing alive.

"How much was the haul?"

"Little over $300,000."

"That's some large money." Leon glanced around the cabin, like he was measuring its worth. Or maybe looking for hidey-holes where Vince might've stashed the loot from long ago.

"The bank got most of it back. One of my partners went on a

drunken toot in Vegas, ended up in a bar fight. Killed a guy. Rolled over for the cops to escape the chair."

"Handed you over?"

"Gave them my name. They caught up with me eventually." He smiled wryly. "They nearly always do."

He leaned toward Leon, eyes locked with his, as if he were telling him a secret.

"I was sentenced to thirty years that time. Did ten in Leavenworth. That's hard time, friend. Federal pens are the worst. Usually, I'd cop a plea to a lesser charge to get into a state pen. I always preferred the ones in California. Lots of reading material. Decent food. Good health care. I met Maria at Soledad."

Maria twitched at the sound of her name. But her hands kept busy, stitching Junior's wounds.

"She was a nurse in the prison clinic. Retired shortly after I got paroled. It's thanks to her that I got out of the bank-robbing business."

Leon grinned. "Put you on the straight-and-narrow, did she?"

"Made me see the error of my ways."

"How'd she do that?"

Maria looked over her shoulder at Vince, her brows furrowed. She clearly didn't like the way the conversation was going. But Vince thought it was the best course. Make like they were all friends here, get them to drop their guard. Then he could get rid of them. One way or another.

"She told me she wouldn't marry me unless I promised to never rob another bank. That did it for me."

Leon flashed his crooked teeth. The boy could use a toothbrush. His breath stank of beer and cigarettes and onions. He leaned closer and said conspiratorially, "Bet you miss it though, huh, dad?"

Vince allowed himself a smile. "A little."

Leon haw-hawed and slapped his knee. "I knew it! Once a

man gets a taste of robbery, nothing else ever feels the same. Ain't that right?"

The *shikk* of a butane lighter caught Vince's attention. Roy was touching the flame to a cigarette clenched between his lips.

"I'd appreciate it if you didn't smoke in the house."

Roy scowled and the muscles in his big arms knotted.

"The landlord's got a thing about smoke," Vince said. "We had to promise not to allow it indoors."

Roy snatched the cigarette from his mouth and said, "You old fucker, I'll—"

Leon interrupted him. "Go smoke on the porch, Roy."

A flush rose under the tan on Roy's face as he took another drag off the cigarette and blew smoke toward the ceiling. He swung around and stepped through the open door. Out on the porch, he turned so he could glare at Vince. He stabbed at his mouth with the cigarette, huffing smoke, rage in every movement.

Leon watched him for a minute, as if he feared Roy would lunge back inside and start shooting up the place. Then he turned to Vince and said, "Landlord, huh? You rent this cabin?"

"That's right. Maria gets a pension. Social Security. We get by."

Leon looked around the living room. "Surprised you don't own your own house, if you were such a big-time bank robber."

"Nothing big-time about it," Vince said. "There was that one big job, but most were smaller. I had a few where the timing was right, and I walked away with fifteen, twenty thousand. But mostly they were just quick in-and-out jobs. I read someplace that the average bank robbery nets a little over $4,000. Might seem like a lot, but it never lasts long."

"I hear *that*."

"I spent it all just as fast I could," Vince said. "It's expensive being on the lam. A lot of it went to high living—fancy hotels, fine restaurants, gambling, and boozing."

"Sounds like a pretty fine life to me."

"Wasn't bad. But there's always the other side. I spent twenty-seven years behind bars."

"Been there," Leon said. "Can't make much of a living in stir."

"That's right. And you've got to start all over again every time you get out."

Leon scratched at his unruly black beard. "And then you got the state all in your business. Probation officers and parole boards and all that shit. Everybody telling you to get a job, when we all know nobody hires ex-cons."

Vince nodded. He'd heard this self-justifying spiel a million times. Every con he'd ever met, singing the same old song. Nobody believes I'm innocent. Nobody'll give me a fair shake. More bullshit.

Of course, Vince hadn't done so well on parole himself that last time, thanks to that asshole probation officer down in Salinas. If it weren't for that guy, the situation would be different now. Vince shook his head slightly to clear it; just the memory of that guy could get him steaming. No time for those kind of thoughts now.

"Try escaping sometime," he said. "Being on the run's even worse."

"You busted out?"

"Vince was something of an escape *artist*," Maria said over her shoulder. "Broke out several times."

He smiled. Maria was getting with the program here, helping him sell these low-lifes on their new-found friendship. Vince thinking: I could take this bastard right now. Brain him with that lamp while he's looking at Maria, snatch the gun from his belt. But one glance told him that Roy still glared through the front doorway. And he still had his pistol in his hand.

"He got written up in all the newspapers," she said. "We've got the clippings around here somewhere. 'The man who escaped Folsom.' 'Bank robber makes another clean break.'"

"You hear that, Roy?" Leon shouted. "Vince here was in the newspapers. He was famous."

Roy spat on the porch.

Maria *was* laying it on a bit thick, but she was right about the newspapers. Vince kept the clippings in a scrapbook. There'd been a time, years ago, when he'd sit up late at night and read them, reliving the adrenaline rush of the holdups, the sweet, breathless freedom of breaking out of jail.

The scrapbook reminded him of the pulp magazines he'd read when he was growing up in St. Louis, stories about gangsters and the lawless days of Prohibition, which ended around the time he was born. Other boys might've rooted for the cops and the FBI agents in those stories, but Vince's sympathies always were with the bank robbers. John Dillinger and Baby Face Nelson, Willie Sutton and Pretty Boy Floyd. Was anything in the world more audacious than walking into a bank and demanding all the money?

Those stories set him on the course his life had taken. His yellowed clippings were reminders that he'd left some stories of his own in his wake.

Funny, though, he couldn't say for sure where the scrapbook was now. His life had changed so much in the past five years, since his marriage to Maria, it sometimes felt like those holdups and breakouts and shootouts had happened to somebody else. As if they were just more stories he'd read.

Vince realized he still stared at Roy. He'd been lost in the past, not registering what he was seeing, but Roy glowered at him, taking the stare as a challenge.

Vince turned back to Leon, found him salivating over his discovery of a real live bank robber. He guessed Leon had read some of those gangster stories, too. Or, given his age, seen bank heists on television. Vince almost regretted bringing him back to Earth.

"Fame's a handicap when you're living outside the law," he said. "Never brought me anything but grief. They put your picture in the papers and you've got to worry about everybody who gives you a second glance. You can't go to the store without looking over your shoulder. I like it this way, nobody hunting me. We live simply here. It's better."

He could see Leon wasn't buying it. He had a faraway look in his eyes as he scratched at his scruffy beard. Vince could practically hear the wheels clanking inside the brute's head. Bank robbery playing its siren song in his ears.

I've inspired him, he mused. This boy's ready to knock over every bank in the state of California. Dumb fuck might get lucky once or twice, but he wouldn't last long. Too easy to make mistakes on a bank job. A bank robber must be smart and quick and bold. These mutts didn't seem to be any of those things. They'd be back behind bars before long. And society would be better off.

"What's your name?" Leon asked. "Maybe I heard of you."

"Probably not. It was a long time ago. Vince Carson."

Leon cast about the room, thinking, then shook his head. "Guess it was before my time, dad."

"Been a lot of years since I pulled a job. Last one was down in San Diego, in the late '80s. You would've been just a boy then."

Leon nodded. "What happened?"

"I hit this Bank of America branch a little before noon, which was my mistake. Too many customers in the place, going to the bank on their lunch hour. Three of them, mechanics from a tire shop down the street, tried to take me down as I was leaving with the money."

"You shoot 'em?"

"No, I fought them off. Had to hit one of them with my pistol to get him off me. The gun went off and blew a hole in the ceiling. The others backed away, but it had taken too long. And while I was distracted, wrestling around, someone hit a silent alarm. By the time I got outside, cops were pulling up."

"And that was all she wrote," Leon said.

"That's right. Next thing you know, I was in Soledad, where I met Maria."

Roy lumbered back into the living room, slamming the front door behind him. He stood near Maria, who was wrapping gauze around Junior's head.

"You about done there?"

"Nearly. I still think this child could use an X ray."

Leon stood and brushed his hands together. "Aw, Junior'll be all right. Take more than that to put down a Daggett."

Vince watched the men, worrying. He and Maria had been safe enough as long as she was working on the kid. But once the job was done, there was no reason for the fugitives to stick around. And they might not want to leave any witnesses, no matter how friendly their little talk. He cast about for something else to keep them busy.

Maria was way ahead of him. She looked right into Roy's menacing eyes and said, "You gentlemen want some coffee? Something to eat?"

6

Leon Daggett craved a cigarette so desperately, he chewed on his fingernails, which tasted of grease and grime. The bank robber had given him the first inkling of an idea, and he could think better sucking on a Marlboro. 'Course, he'd be forced to go outdoors to smoke. He'd agreed with the old man about Roy smoking in the house, so no way he could light up indoors now. But he didn't want to go outside and leave Roy in the house with the hostages. No telling what Roy might do, next time Vince tweaked him.

Leon might be a badass, a big man willing to drop a load of hurt on anybody who got in his way, but Roy Wade was fucking crazy. He was like one of those pit bulls, a wild beast that only wants to fight. Any little thing could set him off, send the rage pouring out of him. When it happened, he went empty in the head, no sense of what he was doing, no concern for the consequences. Leon wasn't sure Roy could even *see* the mayhem and bloodshed he caused when he flew into a rage. Just blindly striking out, hurting anything that got in the way.

Roy had already been that way when he and Leon met in second grade at Lyndon B. Johnson Elementary in Bakersfield. Leon often wondered over the years if something had happened to Roy when he was a toddler to fill him with so much anger. Or if it just came to him naturally, the product of faulty wiring in his head.

He'd learned early on to handle Roy's hot menace carefully. They'd known each other for twenty years, but Leon never felt certain that Roy wouldn't go off on him one day.

Made a hell of a partner, though. From the time they first met, the boys recognized something in each other, a bloody-minded recklessness, and they'd wreaked havoc wherever they went. Taking lunch money away from pansies, setting fires, sucker-punching strutting jocks. Even the teachers had been afraid of the two mean, oversized boys. No wonder both had been kicked out for good in high school.

Being outcast only brought the two friends closer, made them partners for life. Each brought something the other needed. Roy brought strength and ruthlessness. Leon provided a steadying influence. And he was the brains of the pair, though he'd never say such a thing to Roy. Christ, wouldn't *that* set him off?

The only times they'd been separated was when one or the other of them was behind bars. They boosted cars, peddled dope, knocked over gas stations, whatever it took to keep some money in their pockets. Leon dreamed of a bigger score, but the closest they'd come so far was when a Barstow businessman paid them $10,000 to bump off some asshole who was diddling his wife. Leon negotiated the deal and Roy did the dirty work. Hell, Roy would've killed the guy for free, just for the fun of it. Leon at least made sure they were properly rewarded for burying the dead man out in the desert.

That money was long-gone now, spent on rent and beer and food and gas and new upholstery for the Trans Am, and Leon hadn't yet come up with another good score. This road trip, this "crime spree," was just something to pass the time until they could figure a way to make some real money.

Leon still couldn't believe he'd let Junior talk him into coming along on this trip. The kid couldn't do anything right, couldn't pull his own weight, couldn't fight his way out of a wet paper sack. But he always wanted to tag along. When they were kids, Leon and Roy couldn't go anywhere without Junior slinking along behind them. Even when they threw rocks at him, the boy wouldn't run home to Mama where he belonged. He'd just hang back, out of range, and keep tailing them.

Now look at him. Little fucker's got that turban of gauze on his head, looks like he ought to be on a flying carpet or something. His face all red and tear-streaked. Pissed his pants. What a baby.

Leon spat a bit of fingernail on the floor, still studying Junior. He didn't understand how the kid ended up in such shape. Junior had the gun and the element of surprise. All he had to do was get the money and run for it. But somehow, the women in that liquor store got the jump on him, laid his head open to the bone. Swear to God, Junior couldn't do anything right. The boy could fuck up *breathing*.

Maria turned her back while Leon helped Junior change into fresh jeans and a faded denim shirt from his scuffed duffle bag. Then she made her husband get off the leather sofa so Junior could lie there. Vince Carson stood nearby, his hands on his hips, a twinkle in his blue eyes. Old con like him, he seemed amused by Junior, probably recognized the kid was a worthless little shit.

Junior moaned as he stretched out on the sofa, and Leon felt an ache in his own chest—might've been sympathy—and he swallowed against it and coughed. He sat on the edge of the sofa, next to Junior's feet, rested a hand on the kid's shin.

"I'll bring you a sandwich," the nurse told Junior. "You just lie still. Let that codeine do its work."

Junior tried to nod, then winced. Boy would learn to keep his head still eventually. Assuming Junior could ever learn a goddamned thing.

The woman hustled off toward the kitchen.

Leon said, "Hold on a second," stopping her in her tracks. He looked at her husband. "You got any guns in this cabin, dad? Maybe in the kitchen?"

"Nothing down here. I've got a couple of pistols, but they're in the attic."

Leon looked him over, not sure whether to believe him. But hell, what could the old woman do? Come at them with a butcher knife? They could blow her shit away before she took three steps.

"All right then. Go ahead."

Maria went to the kitchen. They watched her go, then Vince pointed to a spindle-backed rocking chair and cocked a snowy eyebrow, asking permission. Leon told him, sure, sit down.

Roy leaned against a bookshelf on the far wall, next to a fieldstone fireplace, using the gunsight of his Smith & Wesson to clean dried blood from under his fingernails. Roy was always careless with firearms. As much as they'd handled guns over the years, it's a wonder he hadn't shot his own fool head off.

Leon noted that Roy stood where he could see into the kitchen, where the old woman was banging around pans and shit. Roy checking everybody, never trusting, never letting his guard down for a second. Leon smiled at him and winked.

He knew exactly what Roy was thinking: They should get the hell out of here. The longer they hung around this cabin, the better the chances some cop might come snooping around. They were only a couple of miles from that liquor store.

But Leon figured there was no place safer than this isolated cabin right now. The old bank robber made it pretty clear he didn't want any trouble. And he sure as shit didn't intend to hand them over to the cops. Man spends his whole life outside the law, he's not about to turn in a fellow felon, even long after he'd gone straight.

Vince had a certain air about him, a quiet dignity, that Leon had seen in other aged cons when he'd been in the joint. Prison-yard sages, full of stories and schemes, not that any of them ever wasted their breath trying to give Leon advice.

This old jailbird looked like he had money, no matter how much he might poor-mouth about his past. His white hair was well-groomed, sweeping back from his face to his collar. Expensive-looking moccasins on his feet. The flannel shirt tucked neatly into his khaki pants at an hour when most men would be lying around in a sloppy T-shirt, slugging beer, and watching TV.

Leon looked around the room and realized the Carsons didn't even have a television anywhere. Damn, what did they do for entertainment, stuck out here in the woods? Maybe they read books all the time. Sure had plenty of them stuffed into bookshelves all over the place. Floor-to-ceiling shelves bracketed the fireplace opposite the sofa. Other shelves stood against the back wall, all full of books. Like living in a damned library.

Leon wondered briefly whether the old folks kept their money stashed somewhere among all those books. He simply couldn't believe they had no cash on hand. Not if Vince had pulled all the bank jobs that he claimed.

He glanced over at Vince, saw he was rocking gently in the chair, watching him, waiting. Something about the man's poise told Leon he'd never tell where they hid their money. Even if he let Roy go to work on him, the old man would never reveal a thing.

Maybe if they threatened Maria, held a gun to her head. Vince clearly cared about her more than anything. He'd changed his whole lifestyle to be with her. Surely he'd cave if they threatened to shoot her.

Which brought Leon back to his original train of thought. The bank robber had fallen into their laps. Blind luck. Ought to be some way to turn that happy accident into cash money.

It was an opportunity he couldn't let slip away. He needed to figure the best way to take advantage. He needed to think. To make sure he played this thing exactly the right way. He needed a cigarette.

Leon sniffed the air, caught the aromas of coffee and frying ham. His stomach growled.

Maria called from the kitchen. "Sandwiches are about ready. Why don't you boys come wash up?"

Leon got to his feet, thinking: Might as well eat something. It'll give me a few minutes more to think about this situation. Get some food in my belly, then take Roy aside, make a plan.

7

Maria stood just inside the kitchen archway by the stove, nervously twisting a dishtowel in her hands while the two beefy young men came to the polished wooden table. She'd set out two white plates, each holding two sandwiches made with wheat bread and mayo and thick slabs of ham fried to crispy. An open bag of potato chips served as a centerpiece.

The shorter man, Roy, looked cautiously around the kitchen, then moved his plate to the other side of the table, so he could watch Vince in the living room. Demonstrating, to Maria's mind, a feral cunning. Just what she expected from him.

"Coffee will be ready in a second," she said, then turned back to the skillet, where more ham was frying for the injured boy's sandwich. She flipped the sizzling meat with a fork, noting that her hands still shook. A wonder she'd been able to sew up Junior's wounds. He'll probably have a zig-zag scar for life; good thing it was up in his hair.

She took two stoneware mugs from a shelf and poured hot coffee and set them in front of the men, who were wolfing down the sandwiches and chips.

"You gentlemen must've been hungry."

Leon, the one with the ugly tattoos, swallowed mightily and said, "Been a long time since lunch."

He took a slug of the hot coffee, then sucked in air to cool his mouth. The other one didn't pause in his eating, but he never took his eyes off Vince.

Maria finished putting the other sandwich together on a plate, then filled a big glass with tap water and carried it all toward the boy in the living room.

"Tell your husband to come join us," Roy said behind her.

Vince was already on his feet by the time she neared the sofa. His mouth was pressed into a thin line. He said nothing as they passed, but he did reach up and pat her shoulder. She took comfort in his touch.

Vince worried her. Nothing could be more out of character for him than talking about his days of bank robbery and prison breaks. She knew what he was trying to do: Get on these boys' good side, make them think twice about gunning down an old retired couple out here in the forest. Make them think of Vince as a comrade. Maybe, if they all got cozy enough, these criminals would simply leave once their bellies were full.

Maria wasn't sure it would work. Worse yet, she wasn't sure Vince wanted them to leave, now that he'd told them his secrets. She knew how his mind worked. He'd think about the future, when these morons undoubtedly would end up under arrest. They'd tell the cops about Vince if they thought it would help them negotiate a better deal.

Vince might lead a quiet, law-abiding life with her now, but he still was a wanted man. A parole violator. He'd done his time at Soledad, paid his debt to society, but the ensuing five-year parole had been impossible.

After her retirement, Maria and Vince had first settled in Salinas, the farm country where her family had lived for generations. The probation officer assigned to Vince there, a fat redneck named Willis, had been a problem from day one. He didn't like the idea of an ex-con moving into his town, in particular one who'd married a prison nurse. He considered Vince an old reprobate, one he could ride whenever the urge struck him. It quickly became clear that Vince needed to get away from Willis' provocations. But probation officers were in short supply in the rural area, and Vince's efforts to be reassigned had only made Willis meaner.

The only answer, or so it had seemed at the time, was to disappear. Move north and create a new identity for Vince Doman, the bandit who'd made headlines by knocking over banks and tunneling out of prisons. At their ages, there was no telling how many years they'd have together. Better to live them as Vince and Maria Carson than to risk Vince getting sent back to prison by some creep like Willis.

Living under an assumed name had been uncomfortable at first, a continuation of Vince's criminal past. But she'd gotten accustomed to keeping his secret. All the Social Security checks and other official documents remained under her maiden name, Gutierrez, the way she'd always kept them.

Maria worked in prisons for thirty years, and rarely had she seen a con who truly reformed. Most couldn't stick to the straight life, no matter how many pledges they made to themselves or their loved ones. But Vince had done it. He'd changed. She wouldn't have married him if she hadn't believed it was possible. Their vows had been more than a promise to spend their old age together; they'd been a last grasp at optimism, a demonstration of their confidence that Vince, with her loving support, could finally lead a normal life.

He'd stuck to his word for more than five years now. Never so much as a parking ticket. But the system never forgot. Somewhere, in a computer or in a probation office file, was a flag just waiting to fly if he had the slightest encounter with the law. Vince Doman had violated his parole, which meant he was supposed to go back to prison for the rest of his original sentence. Fifteen more years, which would be a life sentence for a man his age. Vince would do anything to prevent that, but there was no way for these bad boys to know that. They sat smugly at the kitchen table, thinking they had everything under control. They had no idea.

Junior opened his eyes and tried to sit up as Maria set his plate on the coffee table. She caught him under the arms, helped pull him to a sitting position, leaning back against a fat pillow.

"Think you can eat something?"

He blinked a few times, pain still showing on his face. "I don't know. I'll try."

"Drink this water. That's more important than the food. You need to keep hydrated after losing so much blood."

The kid took the glass in both hands and sipped from it.

Maria stepped around the end of the coffee table and perched on the rocking chair. She picked up the boy's plate and held it out so he could reach it, but she watched the kitchen.

Her husband now sat at the table with the other two, his back to her. She could see his hands resting on the table, perfectly still. Vince always so outwardly calm, no matter what was happening around him.

Maria felt anything but calm. Every time she caught sight of that Roy, a nervous flutter drummed inside her chest. That boy was bad news, no question. Leon was a loudmouth and Junior was a baby, neither of them dangerous enough to worry her much. But Roy had predator's eyes and the physique to back them up. She'd seen plenty of men like him in prisons. In her mind, they were the best argument for "life without parole."

Junior lifted the sandwich off the plate and took a tentative bite. Then another. Mumbled through a full mouth that the sandwich tasted good.

The fact he could eat was a good sign. If he had a concussion, he'd likely chuck that sandwich up as soon as he swallowed the first bite. He was going to be fine.

Maria caught herself and almost laughed. Still worrying over the patient, when she should be worried about herself and Vince. And what happens next.

She prayed Vince would find a way to outwit these idiots. He was smarter than all three of them put together, and probably their entire extended families as well. She'd rarely met anyone with his intelligence, even though he'd never even finished high school. He'd educated himself, always reading, making the most of the years behind bars. He often surprised her with the things he knew—the names of trees or birds or flowers, a piece of music, sports statistics. He was the type of man who absorbed knowledge at every turn. He could explain the stock market as clearly as he could the workings of an internal combustion engine. How different his life would've been if he'd applied that intelligence to something other than robbing banks.

It would be a shame, she thought, if that life ended now, before he was finished with it. But she knew he'd go down fighting with these bad boys, if it came to that. He'd protect *her*, and damn the cost.

Vince was a tough guy, had to be to survive the life he'd led, but he was seventy-two years old. The only concession he made to old age was that he no longer drove after dark because his night vision was poor. He was still in good physical shape, still insisted on doing his own work around the cabin, including splitting their firewood with an ax. But he'd be no match for those two at the kitchen table, if it came to that. Even without their guns, they could defeat him, hurt him.

He hadn't gotten soft, exactly. But he'd been so long on the straight-and-narrow that she wasn't sure he had any violence left in him. And Maria had an aching feeling that violence was coming soon, that it would be the only way to end this surprising evening that had brought crime back into their lives.

Her thoughts strayed to the pistols in the attic. As a convicted felon, Vince wasn't supposed to be around guns, but she'd been willing to overlook it because she agreed with him that, out here in the forest, it was smart to keep a firearm. But she'd made him keep them stowed in the attic; she'd heard too many stories about burglars who used homeowners' own guns against them. Now she wished the guns had been handier when these brutes burst into their home.

She glanced over at Junior, saw him moosh the last of the sandwich into his mouth.

"Good job," she said brightly. "Now just lie back there and rest. See how that food sits in your stomach."

Junior finished off the glass of water, then did as he was told.

This one, she thought as she looked at him, wouldn't be a problem. Too weak to give us any trouble. Let's hope those other two bundle him up soon and take him away.

If Vince *lets* them leave.

8

Roy Wade polished off the last of his food and licked his fingers clean, his gaze never leaving Vince's face. The bank robber returned the stare across the table, ignoring Leon, who slurped and burped between them. Roy thinking: That's right, you better watch me. I'm the danger in this room.

He let his hand drift over to the revolver he'd set beside his plate, its barrel pointed at Vince. He used the gun to push the plate aside.

They'd done eating. That idiot Junior's head had been bandaged. They'd gotten what they needed from the Carsons. Time to move on now. Time for the old folks to die.

Leon's chair screeched backward on the hardwood floor and he rested his hands on the edge of the table.

"That was a fine meal, ma'am," he shouted into the other room. "Hit the spot."

The woman said something, but Roy paid no attention. He noted the way Vince's eyes never left him, though Leon was making the noise. Roy felt he was being measured. It made something hot churn within him.

Leon reached over and slapped Roy on the arm, startling him, making his muscles tense all over. Goddamned Leon. He knew better. Good way to get his brains splattered all over this kitchen.

"Need to talk to you a second, Roy."

Roy's grip tightened on the revolver. Anger fogged his mind and he knew he should go ahead and shoot the old man before it clouded his vision, too. Once the rage took hold of him, all his senses seemed to dull. It was like a red curtain dropped before his face, smothering sight and sound. Better to pop the man now.

"In private," Leon said. "Vince, you want to go in there with your wife?"

Vince nodded once and stood. Turned and went into the living room, moving casually.

The well-balanced way Vince carried his body told Roy he'd once been a tough customer. Fearless and poised. Quick hands and a quick mind. A smart man would be wary of him, even now. Roy intended to put him down like a sick dog.

Leon waited until Vince was standing behind the wife's rocking chair, massaging her shoulders. Then he scooted closer and began to talk in a half-whisper. Roy didn't take his eyes off the Carsons. They were a good ten feet from the front door, and if they tried to run for it, he could blast them both before they reached the porch.

"I've got an idea," Leon said. He pronounced it "idear," which always drove Roy nuts. "We can make use of that old man."

"For what?" Roy muttered. "Fertilizer?"

"Naw, listen. You heard him. He's a bank robber. Maybe it's time for us to move up to banks."

Roy felt a muscle twitching in his cheek as the edges of his vision got fuzzy and red. Leon's blather distracted him, and he responded only so his partner would shut the fuck up.

"You want him to teach us to rob banks?"

"No, what I was—"

"You're crazy, Leon. That old man's gone straight. He'll hand us over to the cops first chance he gets. You let him send us into a bank—"

"Goddamnit, listen to me. I don't want to knock over a bank

myself. That's a federal rap. Who needs that shit? But what if we get the old man to pull a bank job? Then we take the money."

That finally brought Roy out of his trance. He found his partner was grinning ear to ear.

"We wouldn't even have to get out of the car," Leon said. "Send Vince in there, let him get the loot, just like in the old days. He'd probably get a kick out of it."

Leon peered into the living room, where the Carsons remained motionless, then turned back to Roy and resumed his murmured pitch.

"You heard what he said. Even a little bank job would bring four or five grand. That'd be enough to cover us for a while."

Roy's red curtain lifted away, let his brain work again. He liked the sound of that much money, but he saw a heap of problems with Leon's reasoning.

"How you gonna make him do it? We tell him to go rob a bank, he could tell us to get screwed."

"We'll use the wife," Leon said. "One of us keeps a gun on her. We tell Vince we'll shoot her if he doesn't cooperate."

Roy wiped a hand across his forehead. It came away wet with perspiration. Wasn't hot in the cabin, a little cool, if anything. But the rage always left him overheated.

"He could just walk into the bank, tell 'em to call the cops," he said. "We'd be sitting out in the parking lot with our thumbs up our asses, waiting to be arrested. Or that old woman would start squawking and we'd have to shoot her. More cops."

"No, I got it figured. She stays here with one of us keeping an eye on her. The other one goes to the bank with Vince. We tell him we don't let her go until he gets back here with the money. That makes sure he does exactly what we tell him."

"I don't know—"

"It'll work! The old man knows how to rob banks. You heard him. He's done it nearly a *hundred* times. He goes in, gets the money, hands it over to us. We're back on the road before the cops even know what hit 'em."

Roy sucked at a tooth, thinking.

"Even if they get a line on Vince, there'll be nothing to tie *us* to the holdup," Leon said.

"Except those two," Roy said, lifting his jutting chin at the Carsons. "Soon as we're out the door, they call the cops to turn us in. Try to keep him off the hook."

Leon shifted in his chair, leaned closer to Roy's ear. "Not if we don't leave 'em alive."

"Why not just kill 'em now and be done with it? Be safer that way."

"Think about it, Roy. Four grand? Maybe more? It's worth a shot, ain't it?"

"The longer they're alive, the more risks we're taking."

"Banks open at nine o'clock. We've only got to keep them around until morning. Then, bam, we get that money and we're on our way."

Roy mulled the idea for a full minute. Other problems with the plan reared up in his mind, but each one could be solved with a bullet. He saw each objection as a target popping up before him, only to be shot down. Ping. Like a carnival game.

"All right," he said. "But I ride to the bank with him. I don't trust him. He makes a mistake, and I'll cap him."

"Not 'til after he's pulled the bank job."

Roy felt his anger flare. "Whenever I say. Money or no money, I'll finish him if he fucks up."

Leon paused, looking around the kitchen like he was searching for an answer.

"Maybe we oughta both go to the bank with him," he said. "You might need me there to keep you from moving too soon."

"Who watches the wife?"

"Let Junior do it."

Roy winced. "The pup couldn't watch his own ass in a house of mirrors. And he sure as hell couldn't pop that nurse."

"They don't know that."

"That old man can tell, just looking at Junior."

"It'll be okay. We tell him Junior'll watch his wife, keep a gun on her. But if Vince messes up, *we're* the ones who come back here and cap her."

And, Roy thought, if it goes really wrong, they could always abandon Junior. Leave his worthless ass here, watching the woman, until the cops arrive. Leon wouldn't like that, but he'd like it a damned sight better than getting caught.

"Okay," he said finally. "I'm in. But anybody makes a wrong move, I kill 'em and your plan can go straight to hell."

Leon leaned back in his chair, grinning, and slapped his hands on his thighs.

"Now you're talking," he said, louder now. "This is gonna be beautiful."

Roy thinking: Probably gonna be a royal fuck-up. Get them all dead or in jail. But he liked the sound of that haul. Get the money, get rid of the old couple, get back on the road. Let the crime spree continue.

9

Vince didn't like all the whispering in the kitchen. He figured the men were deciding what to do with their hosts, and if it required whispering, it couldn't be good. If he read them right, Roy would advocate leaving no witnesses behind. Leon, charmed by Vince's tales of bank robbery, might vote to keep them alive, which could buy a little time. But how long could he keep a leash on Roy?

Perhaps they simply were quarreling over which one got the pleasure of pulling the trigger. Maybe, Vince mused, I'm not as charming as I think.

Roy stroked the pistol on the table. The boy seemed in love with the gun, eager to use it. He looked feverish, his face glowing.

He reminded Vince of a guy from a heist in Los Angeles. Thirty years ago now. What was his name? Eddie something. He couldn't recall. But he could remember the guy's face. Black curly hair, sallow complexion, a thrust-out chin that looked like it wanted to be punched. Eddie had been gun crazy, too. Vince hadn't liked working with him, but another guy on the job had vouched for Eddie. It was a big job, six guys involved, including an aged safecracker. They got the jump on the guard, got everyone in the bank lying on the floor. Vince worked in the vault, helping the old man blowtorch the front off a safe deposit box that supposedly contained diamonds.

Eddie was handling crowd control when he started shooting people. Vince never did know what set him off. He and the safecracker jolted at the pop-pop of the shots, then Vince ran out into the lobby. He found Eddie standing in the middle of the room, wild-eyed, smoke curling from the barrel of his pistol. Blood everywhere. Three or four people dead, the rest screaming and crying.

Furious, Vince walked right up to Eddie and snatched the hot gun out of his hand. Looked into his glazed eyes, knew the boy was too far gone. No way to bring him back, not before the cops showed up.

Every man for himself. Vince went right out the front door of the bank, dropped the pistol down a storm drain, and kept walking. No one came after him. The cops never connected him to that job. But he'd heard later that Eddie was killed in prison. Not so tough without a gun.

Vince shuddered at the memory. At how wrong a bank job could go.

Maria looked up at him, worry on her face, and he patted her shoulders comfortingly. He wondered what she was thinking, how she was reading the current situation. He wanted to lean down, whisper to her, tell her to run for the door if trouble erupted. But Roy kept staring their way, and Vince—with gun-crazy Eddie on his mind—didn't risk it.

Roy nodded and the men got up from the table. Something had been decided. Vince tensed, realized he was squeezing Maria's shoulders and moved his hands. Better to keep them by his sides now, loose, in case he saw an opening.

Leon, his gun still in his belt, dragged a couple of kitchen chairs into the living room with him.

"Come over here and sit down, dad. We've got a proposition for you."

Vince felt something drop away within him, but he obeyed. Leon set the two kitchen chairs facing each other, six feet apart.

He sat in one and Vince sat in the other. Roy drifted across the room, stopped between Maria's rocker and the front door, the revolver in his hand.

"We were talking in there," Leon began, "about your bank-robbing days. You miss it. You admitted as much. And I'll bet, if you told the truth, you still eyeball banks when you get the chance. Go in to cash your pension check and look around at the security, shit like that."

Vince said nothing. Leon didn't need any prodding.

"I'll bet there's a bank right in town that you've already scoped out. Just in case the ole itch gets too much to handle. 'Course, you've never mentioned it to your wife. She thinks you've gone straight and all. But you've got a heist already figured out in your mind."

Vince shook his head, started to speak, but Leon didn't give him the chance.

"You don't have to admit it now. Not with her sitting there, listening. I understand."

Leon gave him a show-biz wink.

"But see, we need some traveling money. You say you don't have any cash here in this cabin, and I believe you. But a bank job would give us the money we need, then we could all go about our business. And you two lovebirds could go back to your quiet lives out here in the woods."

Leon ran a thick hand over his matted beard, his bad teeth showing, his eyes bright. He was enjoying himself.

When he spoke, Vince's voice was low and cold. "You want me to show you how to stick up a bank?"

"Oh, no, dad. That wouldn't do. We're just a couple of country bumpkins. Take us forever to learn everything you've picked up in your years of experience."

Then Vince got it. His breath caught in his chest, and he had to force himself under control, let the air leak out of his mouth.

"We want *you* to rob a bank for us," Leon said. "Do the job and give us the money. Then we'll be on our merry way."

Vince sat very still. "Why would I do that?"

He caught movement out of the corner of his eye. Roy closed the gap to Maria, where she still sat next to the semi-conscious Junior. He pressed the revolver against the top of her head. Her eyes went wide.

"That's a stupid question," Roy said. "You want the answer right now?"

Vince turned toward him, slowly. "Get that gun away from her."

Roy's mouth twitched, and he thumbed back the hammer.

"Take it easy, Roy," Leon said. "He gets the picture. Don't you, Vince? Last thing in the world we'd want is to hurt your wife, especially after the way she fixed up Junior's head."

Leon rocked forward, rested his tattooed arms on his knees.

"See, we figured you might take some convincing. You've gone straight, you've got your peaceful life. Why take a chance on one last holdup, right? If it was easy, you would've already done it. Told the little woman you were going into town for groceries or something, and knocked over the bank while you were there. Just another errand in town."

Vince watched Roy as the musclehead smiled and took the gun away from Maria's head. He eased the hammer down with his thumb, but kept the pistol pointed her way.

"But you've never done it," Leon said. "You been keeping your promise to your wife. And we respect that. Really."

"Then why do you think I'd rob a bank for you?"

Leon grinned. "Because *now* you've got what they call 'mo-ti-va-tion.' If you want to keep on breathing and, more important, you want your wife to stay healthy, then you'd better go along with us."

Leon looked mighty pleased with himself. He'd need to pay for such smugness. Eventually. But first Vince needed to get through the next few minutes.

"A bank job takes planning," he said. "It takes time."

"Naw, that's not the kind of job we're getting at. You said it yourself: Most bank robberies are quick stick-ups, bring in a few thousand dollars. That's all we have in mind. Just some road money."

"Still, there's planning—"

"Not this time. You're pulling the job first thing in the morning. Sooner we get it over with, the sooner you get us out of your hair."

"It's too risky."

Leon ran his tongue around the inside of his lower lip, still grinning. "See, that's the beauty of this idea. You take all the risk. Not us. If it goes wrong, too bad for you. But you *are* going to rob a bank tomorrow. The only question is: Do we have to hurt somebody first?"

Vince felt a headache squeeze his temples. These idiots. A million things could go wrong on a bank job. And he was out of practice. It had been nearly seventeen years since he held up a bank. Banks had tougher security now. Automatic cameras, motion sensors, silent alarms. Absolutely no way he could get away with it. But he knew only one answer would satisfy Leon and Roy, only one word would keep them from shooting him and Maria tonight.

"Okay."

Leon looked over at his partner.

"See there, Roy? I told you Vince would see it our way. I'll bet he was secretly hoping something like this would happen. Let him get out there in the show one more time."

Vince braced himself before he looked at Maria. When he did, he found the expression he'd feared. Her brows were knit and her jaw was clenched. Her eyes were like black diamonds. She shook her head at him.

He looked away. Surely she could see he didn't have any choice.

Surely she could see he didn't *want* to rob a bank and endanger everything they'd built together. But if he didn't cooperate, they wouldn't have any future at all. Roy would make sure of that.

"Tell him the rest," Roy said from across the room.

"Oh, yeah," Leon said. "In case you get any ideas about double-crossing us, running out the back door of the bank, something like that, we're gonna have a little equalizer on our side. One of us will stay here with your wife. If we don't come back, then she's not gonna be around to fix anybody else's broken heads."

A noise rose in Maria's throat. She covered her mouth with both hands.

Beyond her, Roy smiled.

Vince leaned forward, made sure he had Leon's undivided attention.

"Listen here. I'll do this. Tomorrow. On the condition that you let us be once it's done."

Leon goggled his eyes at him. "That's exactly what we have in mind. Once we have that money in hand, we're moving on."

"There's no telling how the job will go," Vince continued. "I can't guarantee how much of a haul I'll get. But whatever it is, you take it and go. Understand?"

"Sure, dad."

Vince glanced over at his frowning wife.

"You harm her in any way, the deal's off. And I'll be coming for you boys. I'll spend the rest of my life hunting you down."

Leon leaned back in the chair, smiling.

"Now, that's no way to talk. We're all on the same side here. We're a team. You do the job, give us the money, there's no reason we can't part as friends."

Vince didn't blink. "I mean it. I'll do this once. Just once."

"Good enough," Leon said.

He shot Roy a look, and they both grinned. Vince could guess what they were thinking. If he somehow did manage to score without them all getting busted, it wouldn't be the end. They'd either kill him and Maria, covering their tracks, or they'd think it was so easy that they'd want him to pull another heist. Ad infinitum, until they did get caught.

Idiots.

10

Two hours later, Maria lay in bed, fretting and wiping away tears. No way she could sleep. Too much on her mind. Too much anger, too much anxiety. Separated from her husband, locked in her bedroom, not knowing what the intruders were doing out there in her house. Not knowing how Vince might be scheming to get rid of them.

His plan to cozy up to those *pendejos* had backfired. Telling them about the bank robberies he'd committed over the years had given them ideas. Now look where it left her—waiting for Vince to go out in the morning and risk his life, pulling another hold-up. My God, she was furious.

She knew her anger should be directed at Leon and Roy, not at her husband. They were the ones forcing him into this situation. But if Vince hadn't gotten cute and mentioned his criminal past, this might've been resolved hours ago. Damn it to hell, why had he taken such a risk?

She'd helped, playing along, telling them how he'd been written up in the newspapers, making it all sound glorious. She was mad at herself, too. No problem there. She had plenty of anger to go around.

Maria turned on her side, stared out the window at the dark trees beyond, the few stars in the night sky. Distrustful Roy had shoved a heavy chest of drawers in front of the lone window, and only a narrow slit of the night was visible above it. As if I would've climbed out that window and run off through the woods for help, she thought. At my age.

She wondered if Vince was getting any sleep. Whether he felt fearful about the bank robbery in the morning. Whether he might be sad at being dragged back into crime. Or, if he was feeling the old excitement, the anticipation of the bank job.

Damn it, Vince. Our lives were not supposed to take this turn. The past was past. Now all his years of flaunting the law and living on the lam were coming home to roost. You never really leave the past behind, she thought, you just fool yourself into thinking you can outrun it. But it has a way of catching up to you.

She flopped over, turning away from the window, and closed her eyes. She needed to sleep so she'd be fresh in the morning, ready for whatever came. Maybe there would be some way to help Vince out of the mess he'd made.

Desperation writhed inside her. She knew sleep would not come tonight.

Vince sat at the kitchen table, painting his fingertips with Maria's clear nail polish. He concentrated on the job, making sure he covered every whorl and ridge of his fingerprints, then blowing on his fingers to help the polish dry.

"Does that really work?" asked Roy, who was leaning against the back door, keeping watch over him.

"It's not perfect, but it helps. Rubber gloves are the best way to guard against fingerprints, but you can't very well walk into a bank wearing rubber gloves. Every teller in the place would hit the alarm before you got through the door."

Roy grunted. Not a sparkling conversationalist, this Roy. His question was the first non-threatening thing he'd said all night. Vince had hoped Leon would be the one who'd keep watch. Leon was a talker, and Vince would've had to listen to him all night long, braying about his stints in prison and the brilliance of his new bank-robbery plan, but Leon might've gotten careless, might've given Vince an opening. He'd get no such help from Roy, still alert as the hour approached midnight.

Vince focused on his work and tried to put Roy out of his mind. Let the big ape stand there all night, blocking the back door, staring at him. He'd be tired tomorrow. His reflexes would be slower. Might give Vince an advantage.

Of course, Vince would need some sleep himself, so he'd be ready. And rest would be hard to come by, with these mutts patrolling all night long, and with the knowledge of what faced him in the morning.

Vince always had trouble sleeping the night before a job. It felt as if he were bubbling inside. He'd run scenarios through his head all night long, trying to think of any hitches that might arise, trying to plan for every contingency.

He'd known a few bank men who did little strategizing. They'd pick a bank, walk in, lift what they came for, and be gone. No planning at all. Instead, they relied on the randomness of their acts to keep the cops from catching them. They believed in luck.

Vince cast about in his mind for the names of such men. And realized all the ones he'd met had been in prison at the time.

"What?" Roy blurted.

Vince turned his head toward him. "What do you mean?"

"You're smiling about something. What the hell is it?"

He hadn't realized his amusement had shown on his face. "Just thinking about robbing the bank."

"Huh. It's like Leon said, you're all worked up over doing one again?"

"Something like that. It's been a long time."

"But you still got the juice. You can pull it off."

Vince shrugged. "We'll see, won't we?"

Roy's brows furled over his blunt nose. "That's right. And everything better work out perfect. Or you won't like the way things go next."

Damn, he was tired of these boys and their threats. Such idiots that they don't even know how damned dumb they are. They're driven through life by the primitive parts of their brains, like animals.

Animals with guns.

Leon sat with Junior on the front porch, shivering in the damp night air despite the denim jacket he'd fetched from the car. He stoked a Marlboro, practically gobbling it, feeling the sweet nicotine wash through his bloodstream. He could use a beer, too, but the old man had said he didn't keep alcohol in the house; those days were behind him. And the only liquor store for miles was the one where the old ladies brained Junior.

Junior's eyelids were at half-mast, his turbaned head lolling on his neck despite the cold. Leon had brought him outdoors to hear the plan for the bank robbery. Figured the night air might help the kid snap out of his codeine stupor. He could tell Junior still hurt like hell, but the runt put on the good front, acting like he was okay, like he could handle his end of tomorrow's action.

"All you got to do," Leon said, "is keep an eye on the old lady. You'll have a gun, but you won't have to use it. She won't try anything, not while we've got her husband. You'll only be alone with her maybe an hour. You can handle that, right?"

"Ssshure, Leon," Junior slurred, too doped to know what he was saying. Leon hoped he'd be better in the morning.

"I'm counting on you, little brother. I can't let Roy take that old man to the bank alone. Roy can't control himself, you know that. I need to be there. Make sure this thing goes off without getting all over us."

"Roy could stay here," Junior offered.

"He wants to be at the bank. Besides, you know how Roy is. That old lady says the wrong thing, and he'll pop her. You like her, right? You don't want him to do that."

Junior nodded. Slowly.

"I know you appreciate how she fixed you up and all, but you can't let emotion get in the way of what needs to be done. Don't let your guard down. Just keep an eye on her and keep the gun handy. If she makes a mistake, you'll have to fix it. Clear?"

Junior nodded again, looked like his head might drop right off his neck. Leon could see it was hopeless. He'd have to cover the same ground in the morning. Hope the kid was on the ball enough then to handle the job.

"Come on, Junior. Let's take you back inside. Let you get some rest."

He stomped out his cigarette and stood. Got behind Junior, put his hands in the kid's damp armpits and lifted him to his feet.

"You all right?"

Junior's face spread in a lazy smile. "Never better."

Christ. Leon helped him inside, lifted him onto the sofa. He peered into the kitchen and saw Vince in there, working away at the kitchen table, Roy watching him.

So far, Leon thought, so good.

Vince took the seat cushion from the wooden rocking chair and used it as a pillow as he lay down on a rug on the living room floor. The cabin only had the one bedroom, and Junior had claimed the sofa.

Leon and Roy sat together on the floor, leaning back against the log wall by the front door, trying to stay awake. Vince wondered whether Maria was getting any sleep, and it occurred to him that it was the first night they hadn't shared a bed in the years they'd been married. Just as well. He wasn't sure he wanted to be alone with her right now. Not after he'd seen the anger sparking in her eyes.

Problem with Maria was her Catholic upbringing. She didn't go to Mass anymore, hadn't been inside a church in all the time he'd known her. But she'd had right-or-wrong drummed into her by Spanish-speaking priests when she was growing up. In her mind, you didn't commit crimes, period. Not even when the greater good—like staying alive—might be at stake.

He sighed and tried to get comfortable. He'd be stiff in the morning after a night on the floor. Too old for such crap. He'd need to stretch out the kinks, get loose before they headed for the bank.

He ran a thumb over the nail polish on his fingertips, felt the smooth surfaces where ridges should be. He'd done a good job. Two coats. It occurred to him it was a silly precaution to take. No matter how the bank job went, Roy would probably try to kill him and Maria once it was over. But if they did survive, Vince didn't want the cops tracing him. Might be a slim chance that he could resume the straight life here in the woods, if Maria ever forgave him. If they lived.

He tested the fingertips on the other hand. Truth was, he'd obliterated his fingerprints simply because it was the way he'd always worked. Part of being a professional. He'd use a disguise tomorrow, too. Just like the old days. Give himself every little advantage.

He'd have the idiots tagging along, of course, which tripled the risk. Even if everything went perfectly inside the bank, there was still the getaway. These morons probably would find some way to screw it up.

Too bad his last hold-up had to be under these conditions. Given another set of circumstances, he might've enjoyed the adrenaline rush of one more bank robbery. The sweet exhilaration of watching your plans click into place; the thrill of making off with the money.

Vince remembered bank jobs past, a steady parade of surprised tellers and humbled guards and fistfuls of cash. That time in Pomona, when he handed the teller his hold-up note and she fainted dead away. The headlines back in '79, when he hit three banks in one day in Los Angeles and got away clean. The job in Tucson, when he hit the bank just as it opened for business, just as the time-lock on the vault door went "click." Good haul that time. A heist in San Francisco, where he walked out of the bank, a bag of cash under his arm, to find a tow truck hauling away his getaway car. Walked two blocks and hailed a taxi for his escape, calm as could be. That cabbie never did know he'd been an accessory after the fact.

Vince felt a smile tugging at his lips. His body relaxed and his old bones settled against the floor. He closed his eyes, reliving old scores, trying to block out the present.

Sleep overtook him. In his dreams, he robbed banks all night long.

11

Leon Daggett swilled cup after cup of hot, strong coffee the next morning, starting at dawn when a prickly, red-eyed Maria was released from her bedroom. She wordlessly donned her apron and began putting together a breakfast of coffee and pancakes and the last of the ham. The caffeine didn't do much to erase the sleepiness from Leon's brain, and the food only made it worse.

He sat at the kitchen table, facing the array of shiny pans and black skillets hanging neatly on the wall above the stove. The stove was just to the left of the arched doorway, and Leon could see through the living room to the closed front door. He ought to go outside, get some fresh air, check on his car. But he felt too stultified to move.

His eyes burned and itched. His body ached all over. Too many cigarettes out on the porch during the night had given him a sandpaper throat that no amount of coffee seemed to soothe.

Roy hadn't slept, either, and he looked as bad as Leon felt. His eyes were bloodshot and didn't want to stay open, so he went around the cabin squinting, looking even meaner than usual. His hovering was making Leon crazy.

The old lady bustled around the kitchen, making a show of ignoring them. She wore jeans and a white blouse while she washed up the breakfast dishes. Leon eyed her turquoise necklace and the turquoise-and-silver clip that pinned her hair behind her neck, wondering whether the jewelry was worth anything.

Vince had showered, and his thick white hair lay damp against his scalp. He'd put on fresh clothes, too, black pants and a gray flannel shirt. Leon envied his clean comfort. He couldn't remember the last time he'd bathed or washed his grimy hair or brushed his teeth. He could smell his own gaminess. Roy smelled worse.

Junior, on the other hand, was all bright-eyed and bushy-tailed this morning. Still hurting like hell, but the drugged stupidity of the night before had worn off, leaving only the usual stupidity behind. He complimented Maria on the pancakes and leaned his elbows on the table and generally acted happy to be there. You'd think he was visiting distant relatives, getting the royal treatment, rather than participating in a *crime*.

Leon felt like shaking Junior until his teeth rattled, but he knew that was just irritability. No sleep and too much anxiety, worked up over what was to come. He checked the wall clock again, for about the twentieth time since they'd all met in the kitchen, saw that he still had better than an hour before the banks opened for the day. Christ, he'd like to get it finished. He didn't even care anymore what came after the heist. Let Roy kill the Carsons if that's what he wanted. Just give Leon his share of the loot and let him go catch a nap.

His face stretched in a mighty yawn, one so wide it brought tears to his eyes. He blinked rapidly. As his vision cleared, he saw Vince watching him, smiling.

"What?"

"You boys should've gotten some rest last night. You're tired. You could make mistakes."

"Don't worry about us, dad. We'll manage our end. You oughta be thinking about your part."

"I have been," Vince said. "I'll need my gear. It's in the attic."

Roy, leaning against the back door, perked up. "Idn't that where you said your guns are?"

"That's right," Vince said. "They're in a gym bag with the rest of my stuff. Can't pull the job without that bag."

Roy glowered. Leon thinking: Here we go again. Before Roy could start throwing his weight around, he said, "I'll get it. How do you get up to the attic?"

Vince rose from the table and showed Leon a trap door in the kitchen ceiling, just in front of the walk-in pantry. The door had a handle on it, and Leon stood on a chair to reach it. When he pulled down, the hinged door opened and a wooden ladder lowered from the opening. Leon looked up into darkness.

"Up there, huh?"

"There's a flashlight in that first drawer," Vince said.

Leon got the flashlight and shined it up into the attic. Didn't see anything that looked like a trap. Roy stood nearby, watching, and Leon handed him his gun before he stepped onto the first rung. Roy kept both guns trained on Vince.

"Getting crowded in here," Leon said. "Junior, take the lady into the living room."

He watched them go, then climbed up another rung and stuck his head through the trap door.

"It's a blue gym bag," Vince said. "Should be to your right."

The attic was low-ceilinged and dusty. Leon shined the flashlight around, illuminating the pink fiberglass insulation wedged in between the rafters, and a few stacked cardboard boxes, the pitiful overflow from the Carsons' life together. The gym bag was right where Vince said it would be. Leon went up another rung so he could reach the bag, his broad shoulders barely fitting through the square hole in the ceiling, then climbed down with it.

Vince reached for the bag, but Leon snatched it away.

"Hold on. Let's get the guns out of there first."

Leon dusted off the gym bag, then set it on the counter. He unzipped the top and rifled through the contents. Two pistols were near the top, wrapped in black cloths. Leon took one in each hand and backed away. He set the guns on the kitchen table and unwrapped them. Two revolvers, looked like .38s, one with a two-inch barrel, the other a four-inch. Both well maintained and oiled. Both loaded.

"Nice-looking pieces," Leon said. "You always use wheel guns?"

"Never liked semi-automatics," Vince said. "They jam too much. You can trust a revolver."

Roy grunted. He'd made the same argument for years. But Leon was happy with semi-autos. They carried more ammo. Plus, he liked to slap a magazine into the slot, then pop the slide to chamber a bullet, like he'd seen guys do on TV. Felt tough. Felt *dramatic*.

"One of these will do fine for Junior," he said.

Vince said, "Can I look through my gear now?"

Roy pushed past the old man and examined the contents of the gym bag. Not trusting that Leon had gotten all the guns. What a hardass.

Satisfied, Roy stepped out of the way and Vince started pulling stuff out of the bag and spreading it on the counter. A set of shiny handcuffs. Some kind of fake badge. A tiny radio and extra batteries. A gizmo that Leon thought might be a glasscutter. Wire pliers. Two pairs of gloves. A leather holster. Two wigs—one black, one blond. A clear plastic pouch that held fake mustaches, looked like hairy caterpillars. A couple of baseball caps. A ski mask. A roll of black electrician's tape and a roll of silver duct tape. A canvas bank bag.

"Jesus," Leon said. "You need all that stuff?"

"Probably not. But I always liked to be prepared. I'll only take a few things for today's job."

Roy had moved to the far side of the kitchen table. "Why you still have all this junk?" he asked. "You went straight years ago. Why d'you need a set-up like this?"

Good questions, Leon thought. He figured he was right about Vince all along. The old man had never gotten bank robbery out of his system. He wouldn't be surprised if he'd been planning one last job before they came along. Go out in a blaze of glory, that sort of shit. But Vince wouldn't cop to it.

"Just habit," he said. "I like to keep a gun or two around for safety reasons. The other stuff sorta accumulates over time. I see something like this glasscutter in a hardware store and I think, that's just like the one I used to carry. I can't help myself. I buy it, put it in the bag."

Roy said, "Huh." Not believing it. Leon didn't, either, but if the old man didn't want to admit his larcenous ways, even to himself, they could play along.

Vince selected the black wig, one of the baseball caps, the bag of mustaches, the roll of tape, the pliers. He put the other items back in the bag.

"You planning a disguise, huh?" Leon asked.

"Probably not necessary," Vince said, "but I'd rather not take any chances. I've been living here a while. I don't go into town that often, but somebody might recognize me. This way, maybe I can pull this off and still go back to my old life."

Leon glanced over at Roy, met his eyes. Roy's mouth twitched. Leon knew what he was thinking. Old Vince didn't need to worry about the future.

"I'll need one of those guns, too, when the time comes," Vince said.

A scowl crimped Roy's face. "No fuckin' way."

"You want this done or not? I can't go in there, order them to give me the money without a gun."

"Just *tell* 'em you've got a gun. You don't have to show it."

"Maybe that would work for a he-man like you. But look at me. I'm old. I threaten the tellers, they'll laugh at me. I need to flash a piece."

Leon took a step toward them, the three of them standing around the kitchen table like it was a campfire.

"Hang on, Roy. Vince has a point there. He'll need a gun."

Roy picked up one of the pistols, the one with the shorter barrel. He popped open the cylinder and emptied the bullets from it.

"That's no good," Vince said. "They can *see* it's not loaded."

"Too fuckin' bad. I'm not giving you a loaded gun. You might get cute with it, try to shoot us."

"Two against one?" Vince said. "Both of you already on guard? Not likely."

"Still."

Vince shook his head. "I don't like it. I've never walked into a bank with an empty gun. What if there's an armed guard inside? Or an off-duty cop? He sees me sticking the place up, tries to be a hero. You're not going to get your loot if I'm dead."

Leon said, "Maybe he's right, Roy. Remember what happened to Junior at the liquor store? And those old women didn't even have guns. They managed to get the jump on him with bottles of booze."

He glanced into the living room to see whether Junior was listening, but his brother was stretched out on the sofa again. Maria sat in the rocking chair next to him, looking nervous.

"That was Junior." Roy smiled wolfishly. "Vince here won't have that problem. He's *experienced.*"

"Let's think about it some more," Leon said. "That's all I'm sayin'."

"Let's just fuckin' go. Get your shit together, old man. Time to rob a bank."

12

Deputy Debra Kemp put the last of her shift paperwork in her wooden cubbyhole at the South County Station in Anderson. The substation, an old concrete-block office building in Redding's sister city to the south, was twenty miles from Shasta Liquors, but Debra couldn't get Coral and Pearl and their hapless robber out of her mind. Granted, the attempted robbery was the only excitement in an otherwise routine shift, but something about seeing the crime on video, witnessing the women smashing bottles over the perp's head, had gotten to her. She couldn't get the violent scene out of her mind. Felt as if the old women had done her job for her, thwarting the robbery. Made it seem all the more urgent that the robber be found.

No luck so far. She'd fed the half-assed description of the car to SHASCOM, the communications center that linked the sheriff's department to the other law enforcement agencies in the area. In particular, she'd asked Redding PD to watch for the car, since it was headed toward the city when last seen. Debra checked local hospitals, but none of the emergency rooms reported a young man arriving with a bloodied head.

Maybe the perps had driven straight through town, hit the freeway, gotten out of the county. But that boy couldn't have gone far in that condition, not with the way head wounds bleed.

A thought gnawed at her: Whoever had driven the robber away might've just dumped him somewhere. In which case, he might've bled to death by now.

Not that the kid didn't deserve what he got, trying to stick up that liquor store. But something inside her sympathized with his plight, though she'd never admit it. Lord, if the other deputies thought she cared a scintilla about a wounded bandit, she'd never hear the end of it. They'd make it sound like a romance. "Deputy Debby" pining away over some perp.

She'd learned the hard way to keep her mouth shut around her peers. Any gaffe was ammunition for the day-to-day hazing. She was a rookie, and it was part of the departmental ritual that rookies should find dead fish in their lockers and raw potatoes stuffed in the exhaust pipes of their cruisers. If she said something stupid, made a rookie mistake, she'd hear the crowing for weeks.

Some of the practical jokes had a mean edge to them, and Debra felt certain that was because she was a woman. Some deputies still were uncomfortable with women in their midst, though they played a lot of chin music about equality and fairness and the overall competency of their female counterparts, especially when Lieutenant Jones, the shift commander, was within earshot. But some kept their eyes open for any sign of weakness, for any sign she couldn't pull her own weight.

Didn't help that she was still single. A few of the men made occasional smirking references to her romantic life (or lack thereof), as if it were any of their damned business. As if she needed reminding that she had no man in her life. As if working the night shift, four nights on and three off every week, left her any time for romantic entanglements. Wasn't like she ever met any eligible men anyway. Most of the guys she encountered day-to-day were low-lifes. Or, they were other deputies in the department, and she knew better than to mess her nest that way.

The good ole boys in the squadroom would *love* to hear she

was concerned about some jackass who might be bleeding to death somewhere from broken bottles over the head. So she couldn't voice what she was thinking. But she couldn't stop thinking about it, either.

A yawn tore at her face. A long night. Her shift ended more than an hour ago, but she had paperwork to complete and blood samples to tag for the crime lab and all the other little odds and ends that meant a twelve-hour shift usually drifted toward fourteen.

She needed to go home to her tiny apartment in Redding. Get some rest. Hard enough to sleep in the daytime without letting a *failed* robbery get her all worked up. Debra couldn't help wondering, though, what had happened to the injured robber, where he might've gone.

No place to hide in the village of Shasta. More a tourist stop for history buffs than a real town, it was called "Old Shasta" by the locals to distinguish it from all the other Shastas in the area—Lake Shasta, Shasta Dam, Shasta County, Shasta College, Shasta Lake City, the village of Mount Shasta, and the daddy of 'em all, Mount Shasta itself, a snow-covered, 14,000-foot peak, which on clear days floated above the northern mountains like an iceberg.

Old Shasta was practically deserted at night. To the east, a few houses and cabins sat along the winding highway, but mostly the area was undeveloped forest. She stepped over to a large county map that was tacked to one wall, the various patrol territories marked in different colors, and studied the six-mile stretch of highway between Old Shasta and Redding. A few county roads split from the highway and meandered off through the wooded hills, and she knew houses were strung along some of them.

What if the perps had gone up one of those gravel roads, looking for a place to hide? Looking for medical help? It was possible.

She was kidding herself. The robbers must've gone on into Redding. They'd headed that direction, Coral and Pearl said so. Why would they stop anywhere else? But maybe ...

What the hell, she decided, I'll drive out that way, take a look around. Couldn't hurt anything to check a few of those back roads, searching for an old black Trans Am.

Maybe I'll get lucky.

13

Vince checked his face in the bathroom mirror. The black mustache was glued above his lip, nice and straight, and the shaggy black wig made him look completely different. Changed the shape of his face. Took twenty years off him. He clamped a navy-blue baseball cap down on top of the wig, shading his eyes and pinning the wig in place. Sunglasses would've been good, but the day had dawned cloudy and murky, so he'd skip those.

Over his gray flannel shirt, he wore a reversible windbreaker, black on the outside and bright yellow on the inside. The nylon parka was oversized, gave him a bigger silhouette, and it had a hood he could pull up over his head if needed. He put the wire pliers into a pocket, along with the spool of electrician's tape.

He took a deep breath and blew it out at the mirror. Blinked a few times, then checked his steely gaze. Ready as he was going to get. He opened the bathroom door and stepped out into the kitchen, where the others waited.

"Whoa, dad," Leon said, "look at you. You look like a different man."

"That's the idea."

Leon and Roy stood near the archway, already wearing their ratty denim jackets. Junior sat at the kitchen table, Maria using gauze to redo his turban. The bandages she'd removed were piled on the table, stained brown in patches where he'd bled during the night. Junior seemed much better this morning, and he owed it all to her. She probably saved the little shit's life. Yet the larger of Vince's two revolvers sat on the table in front of him, and Junior's hand rested on it, a reminder that the boy would be in charge at the cabin until Vince returned. *If* he returned.

"We're taking your car," Leon said brightly. "I had Roy park ours in that garage out back, out of view from the highway."

"Why don't you have a door on that garage?" Roy asked.

"Never needed it," Vince said. "We don't have thieves out here."

Roy snorted. "Yeah, if you don't count yourself."

Vince said nothing.

"We talked it over while you were in the bathroom," Leon said, derailing Roy. "We're gonna give you that other pistol when we get to the bank. And one bullet."

Vince caught Maria's expression in his peripheral vision. Her eyebrows rose, but she quickly got busy finishing up Junior's bandage.

"I need a full load."

"No, see, we were thinking about it," Leon said, "and it's like this: You need one bullet in case there's a guard in there, or somebody calls your bluff. We hear a shot, we'll know things went wrong. But we'll *both* have guns while we're waiting on you outside. You come out of that bank and try anything, you might get one of us, but the other one will blow your shit away."

Leon grinned broadly. So pleased with himself, with his brilliant plan. God, Vince thought, what a dumbass. But he let nothing show on his face. One bullet was better than nothing.

"I don't like it," he said. "But I guess I don't have much choice."

"That's right, you don't," Roy said. "And I'm holding the gun 'til we get to the bank. Just remember: Junior's gonna be sitting here with your wife. And he's got *six* bullets. You get cute with us, or this thing goes wrong, he'll plug her for sure."

Maria stiffened, but said nothing. She gathered up the dirty bandages and took them to the trashcan.

Junior tried to look tough. Didn't work, but that revolver looked threatening enough all by itself. Vince gave him the hard eye, waited for him to flinch.

"You harm her in any way," he said calmly, "and I'll make it my business to finish you."

Junior blinked twice and swallowed heavily. His hand tightened on the gun.

"Aw, don't be that way, dad," Leon brayed. "This is all gonna be just fine. Junior watching Maria, that's what you call a precaution. We know you're gonna behave yourself. And you're gonna get us a nice fat haul from that bank."

Vince let his eyes roam the room, settling on each of them in turn. Leon's big grin. Roy's silent menace. Junior's twitchy apprehension. Maria had her back to him, busying herself at the kitchen sink. Her silver hair was gathered at the back of her neck, pinned in place by a turquoise-and-silver clip. She must've felt his gaze because she turned, gave him a steady look. He saw none of the anger he'd seen in her the night before. Damned little fear, either. She trusted him. Depended on him to get them out of this mess. He wouldn't let her down.

Leon led the way through the living room, Vince following, wary Roy right on his heels. They went onto the front porch, and he saw his anonymous white Plymouth sedan, his "senior citizen's special," parked out front, aimed toward the highway.

"You're in the back seat," Roy said as they reached the car.

Vince looked back at the house, saw Maria standing just inside the open door, Junior right behind her. She wiped her trembling hands on her apron.

When she caught Vince's eye, she mouthed, "I love you."

He gave her a wink and said, "Be back soon."

She tried to return the smile, but it faltered and tears welled up in her dark eyes.

"Enough with the tender moment," Roy said. "Close that door, Junior."

Maria went inside and the cabin door slammed shut.

Vince got in the back seat. Leon was behind the wheel and Roy sat beside him, turned around so he could keep his pistol aimed Vince's way.

"You want to point that gun somewhere else? We hit a bump, and you could splatter my brains all over the back seat."

Roy showed his pointy teeth. "Guess you better hope everything goes *smooth*."

14

Maria walked briskly to the kitchen, swiping at her eyes. Junior clumped along behind her, but she kept her back to him, focusing her attention out the window over the sink. Sparrows flitted through the trees beyond the clearing and a squirrel scampered up the scaly bark of a gray pine. Normally, she enjoyed watching the neighboring wildlife—birds and rabbits and wandering deer and the occasional raccoon. But today even the forest seemed menacing under low gray clouds.

She turned away from the window as the boy settled at the far side of the table, keeping his distance, his hand resting on the pistol. He looked glum and scrawny under his turban of gauze.

"There's more coffee," she said. "Pour yourself a cup."

Junior shook his head. He had trouble meeting her eyes.

She guessed the kid was uncomfortable, keeping a gun on her. He never would've done such a thing, except that he was playing along with his brother and that other hellion. She'd seen scores of boys like him over the years, inmates who'd been led astray by others, not smart enough or strong enough to think for themselves and steer clear of trouble.

Maria never was able to conceive a child, and she'd long ago made her peace with that loss. But she often found herself thinking about parents and children and future generations. She wondered what kind of home life produced a boy such as Junior, what his parents were like, how they'd let him and Leon go so wrong. Something else had been bothering her about Junior, too, and now was as good a time as any to bring it up.

"Can I ask you something?"

Junior brightened and nodded.

"How come, if Leon's your older brother, you're called 'Junior?' Shouldn't he be the one who's a Junior?"

His face flushed. "Oh, that. It's kinda screwy. My folks, they weren't real educated or nothing. They didn't understand how the whole 'junior' thing was supposed to work."

"So you are named after your father?"

"No. My old man's name was Raydell. I sure as hell wouldn't want a name like that."

"So what's your real name?"

"I like Junior just fine."

Maria cocked her head to one side, waiting. He squirmed.

"See, my folks really liked the name Leon. Really liked it. So they named their first son Leon."

"Mm-hm."

"And they named me Leon, too."

"Both the same?"

"Yeah, except I'm Leon Junior. I've been Junior all my life."

She smiled at him. "You could always change your name."

"Naw. Junior's okay. Heck, I'm used to it."

She pulled out a chair and sat across from him.

"You look up to your brother, don't you? Probably been walking in his shadow your whole life."

"I could do worse," he muttered. "Leon's tough."

"And that's important to you?"

"Sure. What else is there?"

"I don't know. Brains? Education? Sophistication?"

"Like your husband, huh? Smart guy, reads a lot of books?"

She gave a little shrug. "Like you said, you could do worse. Vince is a good man. Strong. Smart. Kind."

Junior leaned toward her, a hard glint in his eyes.

"Yeah, but he's a criminal, just like Leon. A bank robber."

Maria shook her head. "Not anymore. He's reformed. Or he had, until you all showed up and forced him back into it."

He gave her a mirthless smile. "I don't know, ma'am. I think Leon's right. I think your old man's still a thief at heart."

She opened her mouth to object, but he cut her off. "How come he had that disguise and the guns and all in the attic? Didn't that make you wonder?"

Maria swallowed that. She'd been surprised to learn Vince kept that bank robbery "kit" in the attic. When she'd seen what all it contained, heard his explanation, she'd felt last night's anger rising up within her all over again. She'd thought that was all far behind them, part of a past that played no role in their lives. But apparently Vince had been hedging his bets all along. Keeping his bank heist gear handy in case the urge ever struck. She'd thought what they had together meant more to him than the lure of easy money. Perhaps she'd been wrong. She looked away from Junior, tears smarting in her eyes.

"Maybe you're right," she said, her words choked. "Maybe a thief never changes. Not all the way."

Junior stood and came around the table, rested a hand on her shoulder.

"Aw, hey now. Ma'am? I'm sorry. I didn't mean to make you cry."

She reached up and patted his hand. "It's okay, Junior. You were only speaking the truth. There are some things about Vince I still don't know, even after all these years."

"C'mon now. It's all right."

She dried her eyes and looked up at him. "I shouldn't have pushed you about your brother. We all have blind spots when it comes to our loved ones."

With the skinny kid standing over her, she realized he wasn't holding the gun. She cut her eyes, saw the revolver sitting on the table where he'd left it.

Junior caught her looking and scrambled around the table to snatch up the gun. Looked sheepish as he tucked the revolver in his belt.

Maria thinking: Damn, that was a missed opportunity. I should've been paying attention rather than sobbing over Vince and whatever he might keep from me. Disarming Junior, taking him out of the equation, would be a big help.

Junior studied her, suspicion in his eyes. He moved away from the table, went over to the back door and opened it a crack, peered out at the yard, glancing back at her every few seconds. Watchful again, ready.

But she'd seen that he could be distracted. And next time, if there was a next time, she wouldn't miss her chance.

15

Vince gasped when he spotted the black-and-white Ford headed toward them on the highway.

"Shit," Leon said through gritted teeth. "A cop. Hide that gun, Roy."

Vince watched the patrol car pass them by. A woman behind the wheel, in uniform, her dark hair pulled back into a ponytail, her face broad and square-jawed. Her eyes were on the road, and she didn't give the Plymouth so much as a glance.

If she'd looked, maybe she would've noticed something. Two rough-looking rednecks in a car with an older man in the back seat, bundled into his parka. Nothing suspicious about that, he supposed, they could be his sons, driving him into town. But what if she'd spotted Roy's gun? She would've tried to stop them and God only knows what might've happened.

Roy turned around and watched the patrol car out the rear window. His pistol reappeared over the back of the seat, pointed Vince's way.

"See, that's the problem with bank robbery," Vince said. "Any little coincidence can throw things off. If that deputy had spotted your gun, it could've ruined our whole plan. We would've had to call it off."

"We're not calling nothing off," Roy said tightly. "Nothing's gonna go wrong. Not if you know what's good for you."

Exactly the reaction Vince expected. These boys were strung tight, their nerves practically humming in the car. Edgier and edgier as the heist neared. He knew how to control his own anxiety, contain it, *use* it. These idiots would never learn that skill.

"So what's the plan?" Leon asked. "You know which bank we're hitting?"

"A branch near downtown. North State Bank. I've been in there before. It's got a drive-thru window on one side, lobby on the other. Good sight lines. Several different escape routes."

"Sounds perfect," Leon said. "How do we get there?"

"We're not going to the bank right away," Vince said. "We need a car first."

"What's the matter with this car?" Roy said.

"This one belongs to me. Got my plates on it. We use this car, we wouldn't make it back to the cabin before we were picked up."

"So we need a *getaway* car?" Leon was watching him in the rear-view mirror, his thick brows clenched in concentration. Vince wished he'd keep his eyes on the road.

"You didn't say nothing about stealing a car," Roy said. "I don't like it."

"Frankly, I don't give a shit what you like," Vince said calmly. "We do it my way or we don't do it."

"You think you're *in charge* now?" Roy raised the gun to point at Vince's face and thumbed back the hammer.

"Hold on," Leon said. "The man knows how to do these jobs. Maybe we should let him do it his way."

"Why can't we just drive to the bank right now?" Roy demanded. "He walks in and gets the money and we drive off. That's the way it's supposed to work. People rob banks that way all the time."

"Those people get caught," Vince said. "I'm assuming you don't want that."

"He's right, Roy. Just hold on a minute. Let's hear him out."

They passed a sign for the Redding city limits ("Pop. 85,000"). Buildings lined the road up ahead—supermarkets, offices, gas stations, wooden bungalows that had seen better years. Up on the hilltops, rambling mansions looked down their noses at the older parts of town.

Vince instructed Leon to turn at Buenaventura and cut over to Placer Street, which would drop them right into downtown. Clouds hung low over the city, and a few raindrops dotted the windshield.

"Maybe you better spell out the whole thing, dad. Make sure we're all on the same page."

Vince met Leon's eyes in the rearview and said, "Tell your buddy to stop pointing that gun at me first. He's making me nervous. I can't think."

Roy glowered, but he eased the hammer down and lowered the pistol.

Vince made them wait a few seconds, then said, "All right, here's how it goes. We pick up a car somewhere, then stash my car near the bank, couple of blocks away. You two drive me up to the bank in the hot car. I get out, go in, and pull the heist while you wait in the car with the engine running. I come out, get in the car and we drive out of there, slow and easy, no problem. We switch back to this car and go straight to the cabin, so we're gone by the time the cops swarm the area. They'll find the hot car in no time at all—someone will have spotted it—but we'll be gone."

Leon nodded his big shaggy head. Roy still squinted with his bloodshot eyes, his brain clearly laboring to find the hole in the scheme, the double-cross. Vince didn't blame him; he was looking for just such a hole himself.

"I still don't like it," Roy said. "Stealing a car complicates the whole thing."

"I'll say this again. You boys are just passing through. You get your money and you're gone and that's fine. But I've built a life here. I've got to do this right or it'll come back on Maria and me. I'm not cutting corners."

The car topped a rise and downtown spread out before them at the bottom of a steep hill. Droopy palm trees bracketed the street in front of clapboard houses, looking out of place among the evergreens and oaks. Flat-roofed stores and businesses flanked the railroad tracks down below. A seven-story building, a tan stucco monolith with vertical slits for windows, towered over the scene.

"See that building?" Vince said. "That's the county jail. Tallest building in town. There's a reason for that. Folks around here are serious about law-and-order. Unless you two want to end up inside that building, I'd suggest we do this my way."

"I ain't afraid of jail," Roy said. "I've been in worse joints than that."

"That one would be just the beginning. I don't intend to spend any more time inside myself. I'm too old. And I imagine you guys would rather stay free, too, once this is over."

"Listen to him, Roy. He makes sense."

Roy looked unconvinced, but he gave in. "All right. Where do we get this car?"

"Anywhere," Vince said. "Parking lot. Somebody's driveway. Just hot-wire it. We'll only need it for a little while."

Leon looked over at Roy. Vince saw something pass between them.

"You boys do know how to hot-wire a car, don't you?"

Roy scowled. Leon's face flushed. Vince sighed heavily, putting on a show.

"Oh, hell," he said. "I'll do it. Just keep driving. I'll tell you where to turn."

16

Debra went all the way to the turnoff for Whiskeytown Lake's visitors' center without spotting the Trans Am or any other sign of the liquor store robber. She steered into the parking lot to turn around. Rain misted down, and the roiling clouds looked as if they might open up any second and dump a real bucketful.

The glass-walled visitors' center sat on a bluff high above the lake, which filled the valley below, the water slate-gray under the churning sky. Debra suppressed a shudder. The lake was a popular spot with boaters and picnickers and swimmers, but it always gave her the creeps. The manmade lake inundated an old mining community—the Whiskeytown in its name—when the dam was built forty years earlier, and the thought of old stores and houses under all those acres of water made the lake feel like a graveyard to her.

Of all the ways a person could die, Debra feared drowning most. The mere thought of being stuck underwater made her gasp for breath. The phobia was why she avoided working the boats for the sheriff's department. Patrolling Lake Shasta and the Sacramento River and other waterways around the county was considered a plum assignment—outdoors, lots of sunshine, easy duty arresting the occasional drunk and warning boaters to obey the rules. But Debra didn't like the idea of being out on the water. Besides, she had her sights set on detective, not lifeguard.

She sighed as she wheeled her cruiser onto the highway, headed back toward Old Shasta and Redding, and thought that was what she was doing now—playing detective. Working a hunch about what might've happened to the bleeding robber. It was getting her nowhere. She'd driven four gravel roads and stopped in twice as many driveways, poking among the trees that lined the highway, without finding a thing out of the ordinary. Probably just spooked a lot of residents who wondered what a deputy might want on their property.

She gave the car more gas to climb a hill, and the Ford roared as it shifted into overdrive. The Crown Vic was like a trusty steed she rode around the county, always responding to her needs. She sometimes felt as if it were her real home, more than her small, lonely apartment in Redding. She certainly spent more time in the cruiser, strapped into the seat, the cage behind her, a shotgun racked beside her, the radio and on-board computer beeping and squawking in counterpoint to her thumping windshield wipers. Her eyes flitted over to the computer screen, checking what calls were drawing responses from the day-shift deputies. Nothing new about the attempted hold-up at Shasta Liquors. Still no sign of that black Trans Am.

She slowed as she passed through Shasta—never could tell when some tourist might walk right out in front of you. She scanned the muddy parking lots for any sign of the Trans Am. Nothing.

Debra sighed again and blinked her scratchy eyes. Time to give this up. Go home and go to bed. She speeded up as she passed the liquor store. She could imagine what was going on inside today, Pearl and Coral showing the videotape copy of their heroics to every drunk who stopped by.

She drove a couple of miles, steering through curves, then saw muddy arcs left on the black pavement by car tires. Somebody headed into town this morning, pulling out of a dirt driveway.

She slowed, recognizing the place was one she hadn't checked earlier. She turned on her blinker and nosed the patrol car into the driveway. Pines grew close on either side, brushing her car. No wonder she hadn't noticed the turnoff on her first pass.

A honey-colored cabin sat back from the road, surrounded by dripping trees. No vehicles out front, though there was a shed in back, might be a garage. It was turned away from the highway, so all she could see was a blank wall. Lights glowed around the edges of the thick curtains in the cabin's windows, though. Somebody was home.

Debra saw the maroon curtains move as someone inside peeked out. Shit, she thought, I've probably got this whole end of the county buzzing about patrol cars snooping around.

She shifted into reverse, backed the Ford around, thinking: A nice-looking cabin. Tidy. She wouldn't mind having a place like this, out away from town, quiet in the woods. Of course, such isolation wouldn't do much for her social life.

She gave the cabin a last glance as she spun the steering wheel. Two steps rose from the dirt driveway to a flagstone sidewalk that sloped up to the front stoop. The gray stones were dotted with raindrops and something darker, like somebody had spilled paint, dribbled it all the way up to the front door.

Debra hit the brakes. Would the owners of such a tidy place spill paint everywhere and just leave it? She stared harder at the line of drops that led to the house. They looked black under the cloudy sky, but maybe they were dark red. Maybe they were blood.

She threw the car into Park and got out. Felt eyes watching from the windows as she walked toward the front door, the light rain pattering on her nylon jacket. By God, that was dried blood, trailing right up to the cabin.

Debra's pulse quickened and her hand went to the butt of her pistol. She hesitated halfway between her car and the porch. Call for backup? And say what? Residents had blood on their property?

Could be a dozen innocent explanations. Someone had an accident. Somebody shot a deer. Hell, she wasn't even on duty. How would she explain what she was doing out here, poking around private property?

Hand on her Glock, she went up the walk and onto the wooden porch. Knocked on the door. Waited a few seconds. Knocked again.

The door opened a foot and a silver-haired woman peered through the gap. She had shiny dark eyes and a big smile. Wore jeans and a white blouse, but what caught Debra's eye was her turquoise necklace. Very nice.

"Yes?"

"Good morning, ma'am. Sorry to bother you. But I was patrolling this area and happened to turn into your driveway."

The woman kept smiling, but her eyebrows rose.

"No cause for alarm," Debra said. "Just routine. But I noticed these spatters out here. Is that blood?"

The woman looked beyond Debra's shoulder, out at the flagstones. The smile vanished from her face, but she didn't seem surprised by the blood.

"Oh, that," she said. "My husband hit a dog with his car this morning. Poor thing bled all over the place."

"A dog?"

"Yes, Vince—that's my husband, Vince Carson—was turning into the driveway and this yellow dog darted out of the trees and he hit it. I think it broke the poor animal up pretty badly."

"Right out here on the highway?"

"Yes." The woman hesitated. "That's where Vince is now. He thought the dog could be saved. He put it in the car and raced into town to try to find a vet. He felt just terrible about hitting it."

Debra looked out toward the blood, measuring the distance to the road. She could picture an old man stopping his car, picking up the dog, carrying it to the house. He and his wife deciding he'd drive the injured animal into town. It made sense. Debra turned back to the woman, found her watching her intently.

"The dog was bleeding?"

"Yes, from its mouth. I think it probably had internal injuries, but Vince insisted on trying to save it."

The woman still held the door, open just enough to peer out. Debra wondered if she should ask to come inside, make an excuse. Can I use your bathroom? Look around while she was in there. But she didn't have reason to doubt the dog story. Just desperate to prove her hunch about the liquor-store robber, imagining crimes where there were none. She should go home and sleep.

"Which vet was he going to?"

"I'm not sure," Mrs. Carson said. "Probably that pet hospital up on Eureka Way, by the supermarket? That's the closest one."

"Okay, ma'am. Sorry to trouble you. I was just checking."

"No trouble at all, young lady. Glad to see the sheriff's department is keeping an eye on us out here."

The old woman smiled again, the skin crinkling around her eyes.

"I hope the dog survives," Debra said. "And that your husband's okay."

"Thanks, dear," the woman said. The smile slipped from her face. "I hope so, too."

Then she closed the door. Debra slumped back to her cruiser, taking care not to step on the spots of blood.

17

Maria closed the door and watched through its small window as the heavy-set deputy climbed back into her patrol car. The car started up and exhaust puffed from the tailpipe. Then the black-and-white car eased toward the highway.

She rested her forehead against the door, her eyes closed, striving for composure. After a moment, she glanced at Junior, who stood trembling at the window to her left, the gun still pointed her way. He peeked through the narrow slit between the curtains and the edge of the window. She looked outside again, too, saw the patrol car turn toward Redding.

When she turned back, Junior was watching her. His mouth twitched, trying to smile, though his brown eyes were wide and scared beneath the gauze turban.

"You did good, ma'am. Real good."

"You think she believed me?"

"Think so. That was quick, coming up with that story about the dog. I hadn't even noticed that blood out there."

"There was blood everywhere last night," she said. "All from you."

He grinned. "You fixed me up. And now you talked that deputy out of coming inside. You're doing real good."

She wasn't so sure she'd handled the deputy correctly. Maria had seen doubt in her eyes. She might check with the veterinary hospital, see whether Vince ever showed up there. She hoped the deputy wasn't interested enough to pursue it. Maria didn't want Vince robbing that bank, but she didn't want him caught, either.

"She's not coming back," Junior said as he looked again past the curtains. Sounded like he was trying to convince himself. "You did real good."

She wished he'd stop saying that. She'd played her role only because she had no choice. She'd wanted to run out that door, right into the protective arms of that young officer. Let *her* deal with Junior. Shoot him, disarm him, arrest him, whatever. But Maria had kept Vince in her mind, and it had given her strength enough to bluff the deputy.

Junior gestured with the pistol, and Maria returned to the kitchen, the boy right behind her. She topped off her coffee cup before they sat at the table in the same places as before.

"Whew," he said. "That was a close one, huh?"

He twisted his neck, relieving the tension, then looked a little dizzy, his eyes unfocused for a moment. Maria still thought he might have a concussion. Getting whacked over the head with heavy bottles, repeatedly, couldn't be good for the brain. And Junior didn't seem to have a lot of brains anyway. Probably room in his skull for them to rattle around.

"Your head's still hurting you, isn't it?"

He smiled weakly. "I'll be all right."

"You want more codeine?"

His eyes went wary. "You'd like that, wouldn't you? Get me all doped up again, so you could try something."

Maria pursed her lips, tried to look put out.

"That wasn't what I meant at all," she said, though it was exactly what she'd been thinking. "I just hate to see anyone in pain. Occupational hazard."

Junior had set the revolver on the table. He saw Maria glance at it, and he plucked it up, stuck it in the waistband of his jeans. She acted like she hadn't noticed. She needed to engage the boy, make him forget about that pistol.

"I was a nurse for a long time, you know."

"Yeah?"

"Over thirty years. Most of that time working in prisons."

"Must've been tough duty."

"Oh, it wasn't so bad. You get used to it."

"That's where you met your husband?"

"That's right. My first husband had been dead for seven years, so I'd gotten pretty used to being alone. But then Vince came along, and I decided to give it another try."

"How did that work?" Junior asked. "I mean, it's prison, right? How did you get to know each other? Wasn't like he could ask you out."

Maria smiled. "It was a little tricky, but Vince was very smooth."

"Yeah?"

"The first time I saw him, he'd been in a fight, and it never occurred to me that he was anything more than just another troublesome inmate."

"A fight?"

"He came into the infirmary, had this long slice on his forearm, where some young tough had gone at him with a shank. The doctor was sewing it up and I assisted."

"Some guy *cut* him?"

"Happens all the time in the pen. The difference here was that the guy who did it was in the next bed. Vince had broken his arm. Given him two black eyes, too. Guess he worked him over some before the guards separated them.

"I heard this from the doctor," she said. "Vince sat on the edge of the bed, not bragging about the fight, not flinching while the doctor cleaned and dressed his wound. In fact, he ignored the doctor, too busy trying to strike up a conversation with me."

Junior grinned.

"I'd heard such come-ons before, of course. When you're a woman working in a prison, you become expert at deflecting the passes of lonely inmates. But Vince was close to my age, and something about his poise, his charm, that damned twinkle in his eyes, slipped past my defenses. I found myself thinking about him long after he returned to his cell."

She took a big gulp of coffee, watching Junior over the rim of the cup. He still smiled, eager for the rest of the story.

"Wasn't long before Vince was a regular patient in the infirmary. A man his age could persuade the guards he had most any illness, and he faked one symptom after another, each time managing to end up in my care. Always a gentleman, never trying to break prison rules by kissing me or holding my hand or anything like that. Just talking. Telling each other the story of our lives.

"Then one day, after about a year, he comes to the infirmary with a 'fever,' which I knew right away he'd faked by wrapping himself up in blankets or something. He told me his parole had come through, that he'd be getting out in a week. That he wanted to see me again, on the outside, where the rules no longer applied."

"What did you say?"

"I didn't know what to say at first. I mean, I felt truly upset that I might not see him again. But to take up with an inmate? I'd seen too many co-workers fall into that trap over the years. It almost always turns out badly.

"I tried to make light of it. Told him he'd want a younger woman, once he was on the outside. He said, 'I don't want some twenty-year-old bimbo who doesn't know anything. Doesn't remember Frank Sinatra or World War II. Has never read a book. I want a woman who's had the same experiences as me.'"

"Good answer," Junior said, which made Maria smile.

"I thought so, too. But I still couldn't quite believe it. I said, 'Why me?' And do you know what he said? 'Because you're the one.'"

Junior leaned back, grinning. "Ol' Vince is a romantic."

"After his parole, we started dating, just like a couple of teen-agers. Eating in cafes and walking on beaches and holding hands. After a year, we got married. After I retired, we moved up here."

"And lived happily ever after," he said.

She stared at him, waiting for him to recognize what he'd said, how their happily-ever-after had taken a turn since he'd shown up on their doorstep the night before. He got it after a second, and his smile faded.

"So far," she said.

18

Roy Wade opened the Plymouth's door and climbed out into the cold drizzle, holding his pistol by his thigh. Vince got out of the back seat, and Roy stood close to him.

"Play it cool," he muttered. "I'll be right on your heels."

He whipped his head around, checking for witnesses. They'd stopped beside a Safeway about a mile from the bank, near the back of the store, far from the coming and going out front. Vince said it was where the store employees would park their cars, out of customers' way, which meant nobody would look for these cars until the shift ended. Buy them a little time.

Leon had run his mouth about how smart that was, but Roy thought, hell, anybody could've figured that out if he took a minute to consider it. And this old man, he'd done this sort of thing before. Didn't make him a fuckin' genius.

Roy slammed the car door and Leon pulled away, parking Vince's piece-of-shit Plymouth in an open slot a few cars away. He kept the engine running.

Vince glanced around the parking lot, then eased over to the closest car, an old four-door Ford, a faded junker, its gray skin beaded with raindrops.

"Why you messing with that one?" Roy hissed. "Take that one next to it."

The car beyond the Ford was a sleek Japanese number, shiny black, looked like it was speeding when it was sitting still.

"You want all three of us jammed into that little car?" Vince said. "Plus, it's probably alarmed. Better to take an old car like this Ford. One nobody cares about."

The bank robber tested the Ford's passenger door to see if it was locked. The door popped open.

"What if we need to make a fast getaway?"

"If we need speed, then things have already gone too wrong to fix. We need four doors. We need something anonymous. This Ford'll do fine."

Roy felt the muscles in his jaws clench as his teeth jammed together. Old man thought he was so damned smart, always had an answer for everything. Roy would like nothing better than to put a bullet right between his steely blue eyes.

He hated know-it-alls who trotted out their smarts and their educations and their good manners. His father had been like that— an educated fool. Couldn't hold a job or keep a decent roof over his children's heads, but oh, he was smart as hell. Kept his master's degree framed on the wall, right above the fancy wooden liquor cabinet they moved from one cheap rental to another. Always plenty of booze, even if it meant the kids went hungry. His father too busy drinking and reading and pontificating to tend to the real world.

Early on, Roy recognized that brainpower had its limitations. You want to get your way in society, then you need a way to scare the next fellow, something other than talking him to death. Roy believed in the physical, which is why he'd spent the better part of his life lifting weights and shaping his rock-hard physique. He believed in strength and violence and firepower. Predator and prey. The laws of the jungle.

Vince sat in the Ford and leaned over to reach under the steering column. He grunted, "You're awfully obvious, standing there in the rain."

Roy figured that was true, but he didn't want to give Vince the satisfaction of being right again.

"Just hurry up."

Roy checked what he could see of the wet parking lot and the rear of the store. A couple of wide doors opened onto a concrete loading dock, but nobody was around. Cars came and went past the front of the store, but none of the drivers appeared to be looking this way.

He bent to watch Vince again, saw he'd pulled a nest of wires from beneath the dash and was busy stripping the plastic insulation off a couple with wire pliers. Once the shiny copper ends were exposed, he pumped the accelerator pedal once with his hand, then touched the naked wires together. They sparked and the Ford's starter turned over and the engine coughed and caught. Vince wrapped the connection with black tape and carefully put all the wires back where they belonged.

Roy couldn't help but admire such skill, but he said nothing. Wouldn't give Vince the satisfaction.

He wiped rain off his face and looked over the top of the Ford, saw that Leon had climbed out of the Plymouth, waiting. He nodded at his partner, then bent down and pointed his gun at Vince.

"You drive," he said. "Leon will follow in your car."

Said with authority, like it was his idea and not the old man's.

As Vince straightened up behind the wheel, Roy slid into the passenger seat, keeping the gun on him, and slammed the door shut.

"Let's go see this bank."

Vince backed the car out of the parking space and turned toward the exit. Roy checked over his shoulder, made sure Leon was following. Then he settled against the seat, his eyes on Vince, the pistol itchy in his hand.

19

Debra took off her heavy gunbelt as soon as she got inside her apartment in east Redding. With the holstered Glock and other equipment, the belt weighed more than ten pounds, and it chafed her hips.

She set the gear on her round dining table, then squeezed past to the stove, put the kettle on for a cup of herbal tea. A portable stereo sat on the counter, and she hit the "play" button. A plaintive Norah Jones tune filled the kitchen.

The music made her think of Bud, her last boyfriend. He'd hated this disc, called the music "whiny," while Debra found it soothing. In a way, he'd ruined it for her. Now, whenever she heard it, she thought of him, even though they'd broken up nearly a year ago, and she hadn't even seen him in more than six months. Since she'd made patrol, she hardly had time for any of her friends, much less old boyfriends with bad taste in music.

It wasn't just the music that brought him to mind, she realized. Bud resembled the perp she'd seen on the Shasta Liquors video. Bud's hair was lighter and his face rounder, but he was built similarly to the hapless robber. On the skinny side, about five-ten, only a couple of inches taller than her. She'd outweighed Bud by twenty pounds, a fact that had revealed itself one night when they'd had a few too many beers.

That had been the beginning of the end of that relationship. Bud hadn't seemed to mind her round hips and heavy thighs when they were in bed, but he suddenly lost interest when presented with the hard data.

It was a challenge to his manhood, having a girlfriend who was bigger than him. As if the uniform and the gunbelt and the authority of the badge weren't challenge enough. She could understand how a man might think twice before approaching such a daunting package. Small wonder she hadn't been asked out since Bud abandoned her.

She sighed and tried to push him from her mind. She was just tired, that's all. A long, long night, followed by two hours of driving up and down curvy Highway 299 in a fruitless search for the black Trans Am.

She thought again of the blood spots she'd seen on the flagstone walkway outside that cabin, the last place she'd stopped. That silver-haired woman, Mrs. Carson, had kind eyes, seemed like a gentle soul. Debra imagined her husband would be the same. Poor old man, worried about some stray hound busted up by his bumper.

Dogs got run over on these highways all the time. Most folks wouldn't even bother to look in the rearview mirror, much less stop and see if they could help the poor animal. The Carsons must be real good people.

Still, something wasn't quite right with the story. Why would the husband drag the dog all the way up to the porch, getting blood everywhere, if he was worried about internal injuries? And Debra had seen no skid marks on the highway in front of the cabin. If the old man had stopped suddenly, trying to avoid the dog, wouldn't he have left some rubber on the road?

She tried to recall exactly what the wife had said about how the accident happened. The dog had run in front of the car *as* Vince Carson was turning into the driveway. Wouldn't he already have slowed down, to make his turn? Why hadn't the dog darted out of the way?

The kettle whistled, and Debra realized she'd been standing by the stove all this time, staring at a blank white wall. Jesus, she was losing it.

She tried to force the attempted robbery and the blood and the dog out of her mind as she prepared her cup of tea and wearily sat down at the table. But the thoughts wouldn't budge.

Better than thoughts of Bud, she supposed. She couldn't believe she'd been mooning over him, all these months later. Her hormones must be surging or something. Her relationship with Bud didn't merit such reminiscing. Wasn't like it was some great romance or something.

Had been nice, though, to have a companion, a confidante. Bud was one of the few people she'd told about her ambitions to become a detective. And, to his credit, he hadn't laughed at her plans.

She reached over to the counter and turned off the music that had brought him to mind. Better that she spend her time working toward her goal rather than fretting over her love life. The sooner she made detective, the sooner she could go plainclothes. Stop wearing this unattractive uniform.

Debra pushed her gunbelt farther away across the table, making room. She got her cordless phone and the phone book. Turned to the Yellow Pages, all the way to the back.

"V" for veterinarians.

20

Leon found a spot for the Plymouth on a quiet side street, three blocks south and one block east of North State Bank. The parking meter stood in front of an office building with big yellow "For Lease" signs on its tinted windows. Perfect. He stashed the keys above the sun visor and got out just as Roy and Vince drove past in the getaway car.

The old Ford turned the next corner and brake lights flashed as it pulled up beside a hydrant. Leon took a moment to fish a quarter out of his pocket and feed the meter, proud of himself for remembering. Taking into account every eventuality, just as Vince had instructed. A parking ticket would leave a paper trail, maybe tip the cops that the Plymouth had been in the area at the time of the heist. Something as simple as paying the meter could make the difference between success and the slammer.

He walked quickly to the end of the block, raindrops tapping on the shoulders of his denim jacket. Roy was out of the Ford, keeping watch as Vince moved to the back seat. Leon jogged around the car and got behind the wheel, adjusted the seat to allow for his longer legs. They slammed the doors, and he put the car into gear. The Ford was a piece of junk, but it wouldn't have to go far or fast. And it was as anonymous as a brick.

"I saw the bank as we passed," Leon said. "Looks pretty quiet."

He adjusted the rearview mirror, saw Vince in the back seat, pulling back the sleeve of his windbreaker to check his wristwatch.

"Nearly ten. I always wait for that initial nine o'clock rush to be over. People stopping at the bank on their way to work. Banks usually empty out around ten."

Leon smiled. The old man really knew his stuff.

"You'll need to go two blocks and then circle back," Vince said. "That next street's one-way the wrong direction."

"Got it. Whole downtown's full of one-way streets, looks like. Makes the getaway trickier."

"It's okay," Vince said. "The Plymouth's facing the right direction. Once we transfer to that car, we'll go south until we're out of downtown. Then I'll show you another way to get back to the highway."

"Sounds good." Leon grinned at Roy, but Roy didn't look happy. He looked tense and mean, a muscle twitching in his cheek. Shit, what else was new? Leon wondered if four or five grand in Roy's hands would make him any more fun to be around. Guess they'd find out, once Vince worked his magic inside that bank.

The red-brick bank and its asphalt parking lot took up half a city block. Leafless trees stood sentinel around the perimeter. The parking lot wrapped around the bank, narrow in the front and wider in back to accommodate the drive-thru lanes. The lot held a few rain-speckled cars, all of them empty.

The southern half of the block was occupied by some kind of store and an old two-story office building, which faced opposite directions with a narrow alley between them. Nobody coming and going at those buildings either, the light rain enough to keep people indoors.

Across the street from the bank was an empty parking lot and another blank-walled office building, looked vacant. Leon thinking: This set-up's ideal; Vince sure knows how to pick 'em.

He turned right, his blinker going, onto the one-way in front of the bank, then took a quick left into the parking lot. The one-story bank had a couple of tinted windows bracketing the front door, which also was made of heavy, black glass. Leon couldn't see inside. He didn't like that much, but there was no help for it.

"Surveillance cameras at each corner of the building," Vince said, just as Leon noticed the little cameras under the eaves of the shingled roof. "Probably nobody watching, but let's not take any chances. Pull into a parking space."

Leon did as he was told, taking a slot that faced the street.

"All right," Vince said. "When I go inside, you back this car out and pull up even with the front door. I'll come straight out and get in the back seat when I'm done. Don't let anybody block you in."

"Don't worry about us," Roy snarled. "We'll be ready. And we'll be watching."

Leon rolled his eyes, then turned and smiled at Vince. "Go get 'em, dad."

"You've forgotten something. My gun."

Leon laughed nervously. He *had* forgotten. "Give him his gun, Roy."

Roy reached inside his denim jacket and fished out Vince's short-barreled revolver. Glanced around to make sure no one was looking before he passed it to the back seat.

"It's not loaded," Vince said.

"That's right," Roy snapped.

Leon shook his head. "We covered this already, Roy. Give him his bullet."

Roy glowered. "I still say it's a bad idea."

"I'm not doing this with an empty gun."

"You do what you're told, goddammit!"

Leon touched Roy's shoulder. "Just give him the bullet. Let's get it done."

Roy reached into the breast pocket of his jacket, came up with the .38-caliber round. It looked tiny and harmless between his big, blunt fingers. He held it up for Vince to see, then propped his own gun on the back of the seat, aimed at the old man, before he handed it over.

Leon turned to watch as Vince opened the cylinder. The bank robber hesitated a second, picking the right chamber, then slid in the bullet and snapped the cylinder closed with a flick of his wrist. He pulled up his jacket and wedged the pistol into his waistband, then covered it with the windbreaker.

Vince ran a hand over his fake mustache, tipped the bill of his ball cap down nearer his eyes, then pulled the hood of the jacket up over the cap. Leon noticed that Vince's hands weren't shaking. The bank robber solid as a rock, which was more than Leon could say for twitchy Roy. Or for himself, for that matter. Excitement and fear roiled in his stomach, churning the breakfast he'd downed earlier.

"You boys know what you're supposed to do?"

"Sure, dad. We're ready."

Vince gave him a little smile and said, "I'll be right back."

21

Vince felt the familiar surge of adrenaline as he walked briskly to the bank entrance. The rain began to fall faster, the drops bigger, and they pocked against the polyester hood over his head, a reassuring sound. Rain cut down on witnesses. It kept people busy, paying attention to their driving or hurrying to get indoors.

He pushed open the heavy door, stepped through, and quickly checked the interior. This wasn't his regular bank, but he'd been inside before and knew the layout. A mahogany counter topped with gray marble ran across most of the small lobby. The counter was divided into spaces for four tellers, but only two were behind it now. Beyond them, another teller faced the big tinted window of the drive-thru on the far wall. Cameras peered down from several angles, but there was no armed guard. Best of all, there were no other customers. A couple of desks sat off to his right, and a middle-aged man with gray hair and a gray suit—probably the branch manager—sat at one of them. He didn't even look up from his paperwork as Vince approached the tellers.

One was a plump woman with bottle-blond hair and too much makeup. The other was a tall, gangly young man with a prominent Adam's apple and horn-rimmed glasses.

Ichabod had been chatting with the blonde, but he turned now and flashed a smile. Vince stood close to the counter, turned slightly so his back was to the manager, and slipped the pistol out from under his jacket. He raised his hand just enough so the teller could see the gun.

"This is a robbery," he said, his voice low. "Please put all the money in a bag, so nobody gets hurt."

Ichabod's eyes went round and his Adam's apple bobbed like a yo-yo. Vince quickly checked the others. The blonde was busy with her computer, didn't seem to realize what was happening, though she was just one window over. The drive-thru teller still faced away from them, counting money.

"No dye packs," Vince muttered. "No alarms. Let's make it quick."

Ichabod did what he was told. His jerky movements caught the blonde teller's eye and she leaned sideways to see around her computer.

Vince waited until her gaze swung to him, then he raised the pistol high enough for her to see it over the counter and said, "You, too. All the money, in a bag. Right now."

Her lipsticked mouth gaped and her eyes darted back and forth.

"Press that alarm and I'll shoot."

The blonde shook her head slightly, then got busy with her cash drawer, stuffing money into a green vinyl bag. Vince watched both tellers, waiting for them to try a trick, try to slip one of those exploding dye packs in with the money, but they both seemed intent on ending this quickly.

The drive-thru beeped as a customer pulled up to the window. The teller greeted the motorist and slid open the drawer. Good. Keep that teller busy, facing the other way.

He glanced toward the manager, saw the man still had his head down, filling out some kind of form.

The tellers at the counter finished packing the two bank bags with money and the blonde handed hers around the computer to Ichabod, who set them on the countertop.

"Zip them up, please." The skinny teller did as he was told.

Vince scooped the bags off the counter and tucked them under his arm. Then he took three steps backward, his eyes on the tellers, the gun held by his thigh.

He looked right at the manager as he turned to leave. The gray-haired man glanced up, saw him heading for the door, gave him an automatic please-the-customer smile. Vince nodded farewell and went out the door, stepping lively through the driving rain.

The Ford sat just outside, as he'd instructed. Roy smoked a cigarette, and both men had their windows rolled down, despite the rain. Leon grinned widely when he spotted the bank bags Vince clutched against his chest like a football.

Roy, in the passenger seat, was leaning over, trying to see past Leon's hairy face. His gun was in his lap, kept down out of sight, and his right hand was busy with his cigarette. Vince saw an opening.

He stepped up to Leon's window, leaning forward, and made as if to pitch the bags inside the car. Roy's hands came up to catch them, and Vince pivoted, swinging his pistol backhanded, slamming the butt squarely into Leon's face.

Blood exploded from Leon's nose as his head snapped back. Roy dropped his cigarette and fumbled for his pistol, but he was too late. Vince pointed his gun at Roy's forehead.

"One bullet, you son of a bitch," he said. "Right between your eyes."

Roy froze and his squinty eyes widened.

"Throw your gun out the window."

He hesitated, deciding. Vince thumbed back the hammer, and the loud click helped Roy make up his mind. Glowering, he tossed his pistol out into the rain.

"Now Leon's."

Leon had covered his damaged face with both hands, and now he pulled them away, blinking through tears. His hands were covered with blood and the nose looked broken, pushed to one side, already beginning to swell.

"Goddamn!" Leon said.

Vince flicked his wrist, popped the nose with the barrel of the gun. Leon shrieked and jerked away. Blood and snot flung across the car, spattered the inside of the windshield.

Vince never took his eyes off Roy. "Nice and slow."

Roy reached over and grasped the semiautomatic wedged into the waistband of Leon's jeans. He pulled the gun free, then tossed it backward over his shoulder, out the window. It clattered on the pavement.

Vince hesitated. He ought to shoot Roy. Soon as he turned to flee, the psycho would be out of the car, scooping up the guns, coming after him.

An alarm clanged to life behind him, filling the streets with noise and echoes. Time to go.

He took a step back, still bent over slightly, watching Roy. Then he moved the gun and fired his one bullet into the Ford's left front tire. Roy flinched at the sudden boom. The tire screamed as its air escaped.

Vince turned and sprinted across the parking lot toward the alley, the rain chattering against his jacket. He ran faster than he had in years, his spine tingling with the expectation of a bullet in the back.

22

Roy watched through the blood-spattered windshield as the old man hustled away. Mother*fucker*. He couldn't believe Vince pulled this shit. Not now. Not right outside the damned bank. Alarms going. Small-town cops racing here, starved for some action.

He snatched at the door handle of the old Ford. He could grab up one of the pistols, take careful aim, shoot Vince down before he could get away. The geezer couldn't outrun a bullet.

The door wouldn't budge. What the hell? Locked. Son of a *bitch*. He unlocked the door, popped it open, and jumped out. The guns were on the pavement, sitting in puddles, rain splashing all around them.

A cold raindrop nailed Roy right in the eye. He winked it away and bent over and snatched up his gun. He wheeled around, bringing the pistol up into shooting position, his thick legs spread wide, his arm fully extended. And he saw Vince disappear around a corner at the far end of the narrow alley.

The clanging alarm pushed Roy toward panic. He saw a man cautiously poke his head out the bank door, the rain plastering his gray hair. Roy pointed his pistol at the man, who yelped and disappeared back inside.

Roy roared with rage. They were fucked. Vince was gone. The car was disabled. They were stranded in the rain. He felt like blasting the door of the bank, shooting out the rest of the Ford's tires, gunning down every living thing within a mile radius. But there was nobody to shoot, nothing to do but get the hell out of here. Quickly.

Leon still sat behind the wheel of the Ford, his hands over his face, blood leaking between his fingers.

"Get out!" Roy screamed. "We got to move!"

Leon tried to obey, fumbling with his door. Roy bent over and plucked the other pistol out of a puddle. Then he ran around the front of the car, arriving just as Leon's door sprung open.

Roy stuffed the pistols in his belt and grabbed Leon's jacket and yanked him upright.

"Move, dammit!"

Leon looked all around, bleary and blinking, still too stunned to be worth a shit. Roy clutched one of his sleeves and took off across the parking lot, dragging the taller man beside him. By the time they reached the alley, Leon was seeing better, was able to run. Roy handed him his gun and they sprinted through the alley.

A steel door opened in the back of the office building and a fat man in a trenchcoat stepped out into the rain just as they reached him. Roy lowered his shoulder and knocked him out of the way.

"Hey!" the fat man yelled as he splatted against the brick wall. But they were past him, almost to the sidewalk on the other end of the alley.

Roy turned left, the way Vince had gone, running flat-out, and he heard Leon shout behind him. He looked over his shoulder to see Leon's arms windmilling, his cowboy boots slipping on the wet sidewalk as he tried to make the turn. His feet shot out from under him and he fell heavily onto his side, scattering water and blood everywhere. His gun clattered and spun on the sidewalk, slid into the gurgling gutter.

"Goddammit!" Roy pulled up short. "He's getting away!"

Leon shook his head, wet hair hanging down over his brow,

water and blood dripping from his beard. He clambered to his feet. Roy hurried back to Leon, got the semi-automatic out of the gutter and handed it to him.

"Now come on!"

He took off running, not waiting on his limping partner, headed for the side street where they'd left the Plymouth parked. Just up ahead, only a block away.

It wasn't too late. They still could catch Vince. Then Roy would blow the bank robber's brains out, splatter them all over the wet streets.

23

As soon as Vince cleared the alley, he stuffed the fat bank bags and his pistol into the deep pockets of his windbreaker. The polyester hood had blown back off his head as he ran, but the brim of his baseball cap kept the rain out of his eyes.

He yanked at the front of the windbreaker, popping the snaps that held it closed, and peeled it off. Elasticized wrists held in place, and the jacket was wrongside-out by the time he got it stripped off, running all the while. He shrugged back into the jacket as he turned another corner. Now, the windbreaker's bright-yellow interior was on the outside, replacing the black he'd worn into the bank.

The Plymouth was just ahead. Vince reached up, peeled the mustache off his lip, wincing against the sting of the glue. He tossed the fake mustache into a rain-filled gutter. He slowed to a trot, trying not to be *quite* so obvious. Just a guy eager to get in out of the rain.

He didn't look back until he stepped between cars to reach the driver's side of the Plymouth. No sign of Leon or Roy in the rain-slick street, no pedestrians at all.

He jumped behind the wheel of his car and slapped the visor. The keys fell into his lap and Vince, despite his puffing and panting, smiled. Leon had followed orders, left the keys handy for the getaway.

Vince stabbed the key into the ignition, cranked up the engine and spun the steering wheel. The car leapt out of its parking space, into the empty street, the tires slipping on the wet pavement.

He glanced at his rearview mirror, saw Roy round the corner a block behind him. He goosed the accelerator, blew through a stop sign, and kept going.

Behind him, Roy ran out into the middle of the street and drew down on the fleeing car. Fire erupted from his gun barrel and Vince heard the pop, but no bullet hit the car. He braked and spun the wheel again, turned right onto another street, putting a nice solid building between himself and the gunfire.

He turned twice more before he slowed to the speed limit. He came to a busier street and braked for the stop sign. Two Redding Police Department blue-and-whites screamed past, headed toward the bank. Vince waited until they were out of sight, then wheeled his car onto Placer.

He pushed the speed limit as the car roared uphill past the jail, and tried to calculate how long it would take him to get back to the cabin and Maria. Surely he could beat Roy and Leon back there, since he'd disabled their car. But they'd get another ride pretty quick, and they'd come gunning for him.

Then it hit him. They didn't need to outrun him. All they needed was a telephone. They could call the house, alert Junior that he was coming, tell the kid things had gone wrong. They might tell him to go ahead and shoot Maria. Vince didn't think Junior had it in him to commit murder, but he seemed willing to do most anything his idiot brother commanded. Went into that liquor store and tried to hold it up with an empty pistol, just because Leon said so. Even if Junior didn't have the gumption to shoot Maria, he'd still be waiting on Vince if they alerted him. And Vince was now the one who had a gun with no bullets.

His mind whirred as he steered the Plymouth north onto another street, turning right on red, still headed in the general direction of the cabin. The highway was up ahead, another mile or so. Once he reached it, he could go flat-out back to the cabin, speed limits be damned. Every cop in town was probably zooming toward that bank now anyway.

But he might need to make a stop on his way. Just for a minute. Long enough to get some ammo.

The light was green at Highway 299, and the Plymouth slid sideways as Vince wrestled it through the intersection. The tires grabbed, and the car shot westward.

Ahead on the right, half a mile away, stood Archie's Bait Shop, a ramshackle place where fishermen and boaters on their way to Whiskeytown Lake could stop for ice and night crawlers and last-minute tips. Vince, no fisherman himself, had never been inside the place. Did Archie carry ammunition? He sure as hell hoped so.

He braked hard and gripped the wheel with both hands as the Plymouth bounced across the rutted gravel parking lot, muddy water flying from puddles. He got the car stopped just outside the front door of the store and bailed out into the downpour.

The bait shop had a rusty screen door, then a wooden front door with a grated window set into it. A bell jingled as Vince pushed the second door open and stepped in out of the rain. The store was crowded with ice chests and bait tanks and shelves full of dusty gear. An older man dressed all in khaki was behind the cash register. He had a newspaper spread out on the counter, taking it easy on a rainy day when nobody was headed to the lake.

"Hi there," Vince said, smiling at him. "You carry bullets here?"

The shopkeeper—probably Archie himself—was about Vince's age, but looked older, bald and jowly. His eyes were suspicious behind rimless eyeglasses.

"Yeah, what caliber do you need?"

"Thirty-eights. Any kind will do."

Archie turned to the shelves behind him. They were stuffed full of lures and tools and jars of bait and assorted other crap, but Vince saw that he did indeed have boxes of bullets and shotgun shells back there. They appeared to be in no particular order, however, and Archie ran a thick finger along them, his head tipped backward as he read the end flaps through his bifocals.

An old fashioned black phone sat by the cash register, and it gave Vince an idea. "Mind if I use your phone?"

Archie glanced over his shoulders and his eyes narrowed.

"Local call," Vince said. "Real quick."

"Sure. Go ahead." The shopkeeper went back to searching through the ammo boxes.

Vince snatched up the heavy receiver and dialed—who the hell still used a phone with a *dial*?—his home number, trying to keep an eye on Archie at the same time.

The phone buzzed a busy signal. Vince's heart sank. Leon and Roy had been quicker thinkers than he'd expected. They must be on the phone with Junior even now. Which meant he might be too late.

He hung up the phone just as Archie turned toward him, a box of bullets in his hand.

"That'll be twelve bucks," he said.

Vince wanted to snatch the bullets out of his hands and run, but he didn't need the cops investigating another holdup. He fished out his wallet and tossed Archie a twenty. He took the box and said, "Keep the change."

For the first time since he'd entered the bait shop, Archie smiled.

Then Vince was back out in the rain, ducking into the Plymouth, throwing it into gear. Headed for home.

24

Junior and Maria sat at the kitchen table, still chatting, when the phone jangled them up out of their chairs. Junior fumbled for the gun in his belt before he got hold of himself. What was he planning to do, shoot the goddamned phone?

Instead, he pointed the gun at Maria. "Answer it," he sputtered. "But be damned careful what you say."

The ringing phone hung on the wall between the stove and the archway into the living room. Her hand trembled as she lifted the receiver and put it to her ear, said, "Hello." She sounded pretty calm, Junior thought, probably sounded normal to whoever was on the other end of the line.

Then she surprised him. She turned and held out the receiver. "It's for you."

He nearly tripped over a chair leg as he hurried around the table. He caught himself and reached for the phone, keeping his pistol pointed at Maria with the other hand. He waved her away, and she backed up a step and leaned against the stove.

Junior put the phone to his ear. "Yeah?"

"Has Vince showed up there?" Roy sounded out of breath and madder than hell.

"What? No. What do you—"

"He got away from us. Robbed the bank just fine. Then the

bastard hit Leon in the face and took off running. He got to his car before we could catch him."

"You think he's on his way back here?"

"Where else, you dumb fuck? He's gonna try to rescue that old woman."

Junior looked at Maria. She stood with her arms crossed, her hip against the stove, watching him.

He turned away from her, toward the living room, the phone's curly cord wrapping around his body.

"Where are you now?"

"The hell you think, pup? At a pay phone. Had to call Information to get this number, and we're wasting more time now."

"But how—"

"That old bastard shot the tire off the car we were driving. Can you come get us?"

"Sure, but—" Junior's mind reeled. "No, I don't have the car keys. Leon's got 'em with him."

"Shit, shit, shit!" Roy screamed, nearly puncturing Junior's eardrum. He held the phone out away from his ear until the musclehead was finished.

"Now what, Roy?"

"Just stay right where you are. Watch that woman. We'll find a ride and get there soon as we can. But keep an eye out. Vince could be there any minute. Don't let him get in the house."

Junior took a deep breath, tried to summon up some backbone.

"Don't you worry. He shows up here, I'll shoot him before he ever makes it to the porch."

"Yeah. Right."

"I will! You can count on me."

"Just sit tight. We're coming."

"What about Leon? Is he all ri—"

But Roy had hung up. The dial tone echoed inside Junior's

head. Time for him to take charge of the situation. Time to show
Leon and Roy he could pull his own weight. He'd lock Maria in
the bathroom or something, then stand by the front window, wait
for Vince to get out of his car.

He turned toward her, his gun in one hand, the phone in the
other, reaching to hang it up.

He saw a black disk growing larger in front of his eyes, going
huge. He had only a second to register what it was—the bottom
of a large cast-iron skillet. Maria held the skillet by the handle in
both hands, swinging it like a tennis racket, right for his face.

Bonnng!

25

Leon Daggett stood close while Roy used the pay phone, trying to share the phone booth, get out of the cold rain. They'd found an honest-to-God phone booth—you don't see those much anymore—outside a gas station. What the hell kind of town was this Redding, Leon wondered, where phone booths survived clean and intact?

Roy turned in the tight space, saw that Leon was dripping blood everywhere, and scowled at him. They were shedding water, too, and the floor of the phone booth was slick with it. The round red drops of blood diluted to pink where they landed, dripping off Leon's beard.

Leon peered through the rain-streaked glass, trying to see whether anyone was watching them. Not that he could see too well, his eyes squinched against the pain that clawed at his face.

Cars hissed past on the wet street, but the street was one-way, and the scattered cars approached from behind him. His wide back filled the doorway of the phone booth, shielding Roy and his own bleeding face from view. They both still gasped for breath, and the sides of the phone booth were steaming up.

They'd run three or four blocks, turning corners and dodging light poles and fire hydrants, after Roy brilliantly opened fire on the Plymouth, out in the middle of the goddamned street. Hadn't hit anything, but he'd sure made noise. A wonder every cop in the county hadn't come down on their heads. Leon guessed they were all busy at the bank.

He shivered against the cold and took a shuddering gasp through his mouth, still trying to catch his breath after the sprint through the rain. No air at all coming through his nose, and he figured it would be a while before that changed. He wiped blood off his chin and gingerly touched his broken nose. It was swelling fast, pushed over toward his right cheek, way out of place. The skin around his eyes felt tight and fat. Swelling there, too. He ached all up and down his left side from the spill on the sidewalk. Gonna be one big, walking bruise by tomorrow.

Damn. Vince sure had taken him by surprise. Leon had been so busy anticipating the loot, he'd let his guard down. He couldn't believe it, that old man getting away like that, running off through the rain. What was Vince thinking? If he'd just handed over the money, stuck to the fucking program, the Carsons might've survived the day.

Not now, though. Roy had been hot to kill the old couple from the get-go. Leon had been undecided, but Vince breaking his nose had taken care of that. Anger roiled within him. They'd kill Vince and Maria for sure now. And they'd make it slow.

Roy screamed into the phone some more. Leon wasn't listening. He was looking around, trying to figure what to do next. They needed to get to that cabin as fast as possible. Junior had been warned now, but, hell, they couldn't count on him. Vince had outsmarted both of them outside the bank, even though they had the drop on him, even though he only had one bullet. What kind of chance would that idiot Junior stand?

Roy cursed and slammed the receiver against the phone a couple of times, finally hanging it up. Leon backed out of the phone booth to give Roy room to exit.

"Vince back there yet?" His voice sounded thick in his own ears. Sounded like he had a cold.

"Not yet, but you know that's where he's headed." Roy stepped out into the drizzle. "We need a car."

Right on cue, a little two-door Toyota pulled into the gas station parking lot, its headlights on, windshield wipers going like sixty even though the rain was letting up. The dark blue car stopped beside the gas pumps.

Roy and Leon looked at the ten-year-old car, then at each other. Roy gave a curt nod and stalked toward the car, Leon limping along behind him.

A middle-aged Asian fellow with black-rimmed glasses got out from behind the wheel. He wore a green raincoat, but a free-standing awning over the gas pumps kept him nice and dry. He reached for the nearest nozzle, but froze when he saw the two soaked bruisers approaching.

Roy pulled his revolver from his belt and pointed it at the little guy's face.

"Gimme the keys!"

The Asian shook his head involuntarily, his mouth gaping, his glasses slipping down his nose.

Leon veered left, headed for the passenger door. He didn't like letting Roy drive, but hell, he could barely see. Better to let Roy take the wheel this time. They were in a hurry.

Roy slapped the pistol against the Asian's head, spinning him halfway around. Hit him again in the back of the head and the man went down. Roy bent over and his arm flailed up and down as he pistol-whipped the fallen man.

Leon, folding himself into the passenger seat, spotted the keys dangling from the ignition. The key chain was decorated with a plastic yellow smiley face. He sighed and leaned across the car, rolled the driver's side window down a few inches.

"The keys are in here, Roy. Stop beating that boy and let's go, dammit."

Somebody yelled from the doorway of the gas station. Roy

yanked open the car door and squeezed into the front seat behind the wheel. He cranked the engine and threw the little car into gear. Burned rubber as the car leaped forward. The car swerved sideways as it hit the wet pavement, but he spun the wheel, got it under control.

"Go, go," Leon said thickly.

"I'm going!"

"Well, go faster, goddamnit. Vince is probably back there by now." Leon pulled his wet pistol from his waistband and jacked the slide, checking whether the water had ruined the gun.

"Whose fault is that?" Roy yelled as he revved the car through a turn. "If you hadn't had your head up your ass, he wouldn't have gotten away at all!"

"Me? You're the one threw our guns out the window. Why didn't you shoot him?"

"He had the drop on me," Roy said through clenched teeth. "Never took that gun off me except when he was busy smashing your face with it."

"He only had the one bullet!"

"I didn't want him putting a hole in me with it. Once he cold-cocked you, we didn't have him outnumbered anymore."

"Yeah, but you could've—"

"I coulda been shot, that's what. And then where would we be? Cops crawling all over the place and both of us too fucked up to run off. You think you could've gotten away on your own? You couldn't fuckin' *see*!"

Leon said nothing. Roy was right, of course, and arguing wasn't helping matters.

"Then you go falling on your ass," Roy said. "We coulda caught that old man if you coulda kept your feet under you."

"Not my fault the sidewalk was wet."

Roy smoldered, his chin jutting. "This whole thing's your fault. I would've shot those people last night and none of this would've happened."

"Yeah? Well, we never would've *met* them if you hadn't sent Junior into that liquor store without any bullets. That's where this all started. And it's been a goat-fuck ever since."

A cop car roared past them, headed in the other direction, and they fell silent while Roy slowed and watched the mirrors to make sure it kept going. Then he goosed the accelerator again. The little car shuddered as it sped up.

Leon breathed heavily through his mouth, his mind working against the pain. Roy still seethed, and Leon thought he should say something, smooth things over somehow. Roy needed to get his shit together before they reached that cabin.

"We can still get that money."

"Fuck the money," Roy said through clenched teeth. "I just want to kill that bastard."

Leon disagreed. They needed that loot. But he said, "Okay, Roy."

26

Maria wiped tears from her eyes with the back of her hand, cursing herself for crying at a time like this. She needed to see what she was doing. Yes, she was worried about Vince, but weeping wouldn't do him any good.

She wrapped the gray duct tape tightly around Junior's wrists, smoothing down the edges. He'd landed on his face after she hit him with the skillet, and it had been easy enough to pin his arms behind him. And the duct tape had been handy, right there in the kitchen's "junk drawer."

Junior groaned. Blood was smeared on his face, and a little puddle had pooled on the floor where it leaked out of his nose. The boy was coming to, and he was in for a surprise.

Maria took a shuddering breath, still trying to get herself under control. She crab-walked to Junior's feet and began binding them together. He wasn't going anywhere. She'd see to that.

She'd heard what he said on the phone, how he'd shoot Vince if he showed up at the cabin. This little shit. Thinking he could snipe at her husband, kill him while Vince was trying to come to her rescue. She'd be damned if she'd put up with that.

From what she'd heard of Junior's end of the telephone conversation, it was clear Vince somehow had gotten free of the other two. She wished he'd go straight to the police, get them involved, but that didn't sound like Vince. He was a do-it-yourself guy. He'd come back to the cabin, looking for a way to outwit Junior.

Well, Vince was in for a surprise, too. Rushing back here to save her. She'd already saved herself.

She used her teeth to tear off another strip of duct tape, thinking: Most women her age wouldn't have the teeth to do this job. They'd yank their dentures right out. But Maria had always taken good care of her teeth, along with her overall health, and now she was glad. She felt a twinge in her knee, and shifted her position where she squatted over him. How many women her age could tie up a boy like this? How many would have the guts to knock him out in the first place?

She'd taken a chance, braining him with that skillet while he was distracted by the phone. If he'd turned around a second sooner, seen her coming, she might be the one lying on the floor and bleeding now.

Junior groaned again. Maria wondered whether she needed to put tape over his mouth, too, to keep him quiet. But his nose had been flattened by the frying pan, and she was pretty sure he couldn't breathe through it. She didn't want to suffocate him, though the notion was tempting.

She heard a car turn off the highway, the familiar crackle of gravel and the thudding of tires on the rutted driveway. Her breath caught in her throat. Would that be Vince now? Or would it be Leon and Roy, come back to finish her? Had they already caught Vince? Was he still alive?

Maria creaked to her feet and hurried over to the pistol, which lay on the floor where Junior dropped it when she knocked him cold. She picked it up and weighed it in her hand.

She'd shot this pistol before; Vince had taken her out in the country a couple of times to plink at beer cans. He'd said it was to familiarize her with the guns, in case she ever needed to use one. Seemed silly to her at the time, but now she was glad. She clutched the gun tighter and hurried through the living room to one of the front windows.

Maria stood to the side of the window and used the barrel of the pistol to gently push the curtains aside an inch so she could peek out.

Their white Plymouth sat in the driveway, back among the dripping trees. The rain had nearly stopped now, but the car's windshield wipers still flapped back and forth. Hard to see inside, but it looked like Vince behind the wheel, still wearing the wig and the baseball cap and a bright yellow parka. His hands were above the steering wheel, loading a pistol. Best of all, he was alone.

Tears flooded her eyes again, and a happy throb welled up within her. She hurried over to the door and threw it open.

The car crept forward, Vince looking all around the cabin and the surrounding woods. Maria looked, too, scanning the forest for any sign of the other two. But all seemed quiet.

The car stopped and Vince's door popped open and he climbed out warily.

"Relax, honey," she called, her voice choked with emotion. "Junior's out cold."

A smile split his face. "You're all right?"

"Yes, yes. Now that I know you're still alive."

She hurried down the steps and fell into his arms, laughing through her tears at the awkward way they embraced—each of them still holding a pistol.

"Look at us," she said into his shoulder. "Bonnie and Clyde."

He grasped her shoulders, leaned back to look into her eyes. "You're sure you're okay?"

She nodded and wiped at her eyes some more.

"The other two called here," she said. "Told Junior you'd gotten away from them. He was distracted. I hit him with a skillet."

Vince smiled. "Damn. I would've liked to have seen that."

"I tied him up with duct tape. Wrists and ankles."

"Good idea."

She looked past his shoulder, out toward the highway. "Leon and Roy are coming?"

"Any minute now, unless the cops got them already."

"Then we'd better get right back in this car," she said. "Get out of here."

"You go. I'm staying here."

"I'm not leaving you again. We should both go."

He studied her a second, then said, "Those boys are pissed. If we run, no telling what they'll do. They might burn down the cabin."

"Better that than killing us."

"No one has to get killed," he said. "I've got a plan."

She searched his face, finding no fear, no apparent concern at all. God, he was the most outwardly calm man she'd ever known. Infuriatingly so, at times.

"Then we should call the police," she said. "Let them handle it. It's too risky—"

He shook his head. "If we get the police involved, then our aliases are blown. Once they know who I am, they'll send me back to prison."

"But you didn't do anything. It was all these boys—"

"I'm still a parole violator," he said. "And today I robbed a bank."

She gasped, blinded again by tears. "Oh, no, Vince."

"I didn't have any choice, did I? But I got away while those two morons were waiting for their loot. I've still got it."

He peeled open his windbreaker, showed her a vinyl bank bag in the inside pocket.

She clapped a hand over her gaping mouth.

"They'll want this money," he said. "And they'll want Junior. We can try to cut a deal."

"I don't know, Vince. These boys seem too vicious for that."

"Too damned dumb, you mean. But we can try it. We'll hole up inside the house. If they refuse to talk, there'll still be time to call the cops."

She glanced past him again. A car zoomed by on the highway.

"We need to get inside," he said.

"But—"

"Trust me, hon."

She had a sinking feeling, but she nodded and turned away, back toward the cabin. Her mind reeled with the danger, the foolhardiness of what Vince had planned. Why did he insist on facing down these bad boys? Shouldn't they run away? Shouldn't they call the police?

She remembered something, and turned back. Vince held the Plymouth's open door, looked as if he were about to duck back inside the car.

"A cop came by here," she said. "A sheriff's deputy. A young woman."

That froze him in place. "Jesus. What did she want?"

"She saw blood out here on the sidewalk. I told her you'd run over a dog and carried it into town to the vet."

"She bought that?"

"Seemed to."

"Where was Junior?"

"Just out of sight. Holding this gun on me."

A garbled shout came from inside the house.

"That him now?" Vince asked.

"Guess he woke up."

"Do I need to go in there and shoot him?"

Maria opened her mouth to protest, then saw a smile pulling at the corners of his mouth.

"Not funny, Vince."

"Go keep an eye on him. I'll hide the car, then I'll meet you in the kitchen."

She hesitated, blinking back tears.

"It'll be all right," he said. "I promise."

Maria hurried into the house, her heart thumping in her chest, the gun heavy in her hand.

27

Vince pulled the Plymouth around the back of the cabin and hid it behind the open-front garage, which still held Leon's Trans Am. Not a perfect solution, but it would screen the car from the highway. Let Leon and Roy wonder a little when they arrived. Might give Vince a tiny advantage. He'd need every edge he could get.

He thought about Maria, how she still could surprise him after all these years. A fine woman, brave. He wished he'd tried harder to persuade her to leave. If things went wrong with these assholes, he'd be putting her squarely into danger. Could he live with that decision?

Maria met him at the back door, her gun still in her hand, and let him into the warm kitchen. Junior lay near the doorway to the living room, squirming against the duct tape that wrapped him tightly. The floor and Junior's face and his bandages all were smeared with blood.

"Damn, baby," Vince said. "You laid that boy out."

"Just giving him what he deserves."

Junior spat blood and glared at them. "You two are gonna get what you deserve, soon as Leon gets back here."

Vince stepped across the kitchen and squatted near Junior's head. Pressed the barrel of the pistol between his eyebrows. Junior went cross-eyed as he tried to look at the gun.

"Shut up, boy. I've had enough of you and your pals. If you do just like I tell you, you might live 'til tomorrow."

Junior nodded against the gun. Vince stood and backed away. He found Maria frowning at him, worry in her dark eyes.

He still held the car keys in his other hand, and he dangled them before her face. "Listen. Why don't you take the car and get out of here? Head toward town. You can call here in a little while, see if it's safe to come home."

"I'm not leaving you here to face them alone."

"But if there's shooting—"

"If there's shooting," she said, her jaw jutting, "then you'll be outnumbered without me. I'm staying."

He stared at her a long time, trying to formulate a better argument, but he could see she would not be swayed.

"You remember how to fire that pistol?" he said finally. "The way I showed you?"

"My God, Vince, I couldn't shoot at a person."

"Then don't think of them that way. They're animals. Like rabid dogs. Sometimes, all you can do is put an animal down."

She pressed her lips together, then said, "I'll go keep watch." She hurried into the living room, headed for the front windows.

Junior grumbled, and Vince said, "Stay quiet, boy, or I'll turn her loose on you again."

He dumped the money bags on the kitchen counter, and slipped the revolver into his belt. He went into the bedroom, stripped off the wet jacket and tossed it aside. Pulled off the hat and the wig and stashed them in the closet. His hair was damp with sweat and he ran his hands through it to get it off his forehead, then returned to the kitchen.

His legs throbbed from the unaccustomed sprinting earlier, but he shut out the pain. He could rest up later, after this was over.

Vince bent over to grab Junior and move him. But before he could, he heard a car pulling up outside.

He looked through the archway, saw Maria at the far end of the living room, peering out the window. She turned to him, shaking her head, and said, "You're not going to believe this."

He hustled toward her, thinking: Now what?

28

Deputy Debra Kemp yawned as she wheeled her cruiser into the cabin's muddy driveway. She'd called half a dozen veterinary clinics, all the ones on Redding's west side, and none had reported an older man bringing in a dog that had been hit by a car.

Debra now thought that nice old lady, with her sweet smile and her silvery hair, had lied about the accident. But why? What could she be hiding?

One answer kept flashing in her mind: The blood on that sidewalk hadn't come from a dog. It had come from the liquor-store robber, from the wounds Coral and Pearl had inflicted in their videotaped bottle-bashing.

Her theory was a long shot, so slim she wouldn't even radio for backup for fear she'd end up looking like a fool. If she was wrong, she'd never live it down. But if she got lucky, if the robbers *had* visited the Carsons, she might be able to track them down. If she could catch them, it might be just the ticket to get the sheriff's attention, speed her along toward a promotion.

Ha. Then let her colleagues tease her all they wanted. She'd be Deputy Debby no longer. She'd be Detective Debra Kemp. And they could kiss her ass.

She stopped her cruiser in the driveway and carefully scanned the forest and the cabin before killing the engine. No sign of anybody in the woods. No cars around. If the robbers had been here, they likely were long-gone by now. Still, she'd take care approaching the cabin.

She kept her hand on her sidearm as she eased up to the porch, her eyes darting back and forth in search of any sign of trouble. The rain had washed away most of the blood, but she could still see polka-dot stains here and there on the flagstones, proof she hadn't dreamed the whole damned thing.

Debra knocked on the door, then stepped to one side, just in case. Nothing happened for nearly a minute, and she was about to knock again, when the latch clicked and the door was opened by Mrs. Carson.

"Hi there," Debra said. "Did your husband get back yet?"

"Yes, he's here." Mrs. Carson looked puzzled. "Did you need to see him?"

"If it wouldn't be too much trouble."

She shrugged and swung the door open wide. "Vince? That deputy would like to talk to you."

Debra saw a white-haired man dressed in black pants and a gray shirt, sitting on a leather sofa, a hardcover book open in his lap. More books lined shelves on the wall by the stone fireplace and on the far wall. Oval rag rugs sat here and there on the hardwood floor. The overstuffed furniture looked old, but comfortable. A nice room, warm and friendly.

Vince Carson stood as Debra came into the house, one finger holding his place in the book. His white eyebrows were raised, and Debra saw that his eyes were a penetrating blue. He looked smart and dignified, reminded her of an English professor she'd admired when she attended Shasta College.

"Yes?"

The man's poise made Debra feel awkward. She stuttered through a greeting and told him she had a few questions and plopped down in a wooden rocking chair he offered.

"Would you like some coffee?" Mrs. Carson asked.

"No, thank you. This should only take a minute."

"I could use a cup, hon," Vince said, and Debra watched his wife scurry off to the kitchen, sidestepping a throw rug just inside the door as she went.

Vince cleared his throat. He was back on the couch, the book in his lap, waiting. Debra noticed that his pants were damp from the morning rain, and wondered why he hadn't bothered to change when he came indoors.

"I was by here earlier," she said. "Saw the blood outside. Your wife told me you'd run over a dog?"

"Just brushed it with the bumper," he said evenly. "But I guess he was hurt inside. Poor thing died before I could get him into town for help."

"Oh. That's why I came back by. I checked with some vets and nobody had seen you come in."

The white eyebrows rode up his furrowed forehead again. "Seems you went to a lot of trouble over a dog."

"Well, I had another—" Debra caught herself. Suddenly, all her suspicions seemed ludicrous. "It's a long story. But you didn't make it to a vet, huh?"

"No. I had the dog in the back seat. I heard the rattle when he died, and could see there was no point in going any farther."

"Where did you go then?"

Vince Carson still looked perplexed, and she knew he wanted to know why she asked.

"Took him out past the lake," he said. "I've got a friend out there, has a lot of land. He said he'd bury the dog for me."

"Dead dogs really aren't supposed to be buried that way," she said. "You're supposed to call county Animal Control and have them dispose of the body."

He shrugged. "I didn't know that. I just did what seemed right. Is it a crime to bury a dead dog?"

"Not exactly. It's just—"

Debra paused. Sounded like a car was stopping out on the highway, maybe pulling into the driveway. She'd like to look out the window, see who it was, but she was facing the kitchen and the windows were behind her. Besides, she remembered, the maroon curtains had been closed.

Vince Carson kept talking. "I felt bad about the dog, but there wasn't really anything I could do. He ran right out in front of me. Came out of the trees."

If there were more noises from outside, Debra couldn't tell. The old man talked over it.

"He wasn't wearing a collar, so I assumed he was a stray. Though what he was doing way out here in our woods, I couldn't say."

Mrs. Carson came back from the kitchen, carrying a steaming mug. The coffee smelled wonderful, and Debra swallowed against the saliva that filled her mouth. She wished she'd accepted a cup after all, though caffeine was the last thing she needed right now. She should go home, go to bed. No way to check out the old couple's story, not unless she wanted to drive out past the lake and visit the friend he'd mentioned. And Debra couldn't see herself doing that. Hadn't this craziness gone far enough?

"Don't worry about it," she said. "Sounds like you did everything humanly possible to help the animal."

"I tried."

Debra slapped her round knees and got to her feet. "Okay, then. Guess I'll get a move-on."

Vince Carson stood, too, the coffee in one hand, the book in the other.

"Thanks for stopping by," he said. "It's good to see the sheriff's department is so interested in what goes on out in this part of the county."

"Sure," Debra said. She went to the front door and flung it open, the Carsons right on her heels. She looked outside, past the dripping eaves of the porch. Her cruiser was the only car in the driveway.

"I thought I heard a car out here," she said.

"Probably just highway noise," Mrs. Carson said. "We hear passing cars a lot better when the pavement's wet."

Debra nodded and walked down off the porch. The old couple stood in the doorway, watching her go. She stifled a yawn as she got behind the wheel of her cruiser. She checked her rearview, saw the Carsons had gone back inside. The door was closed.

She shook her head at her own foolishness, and steered toward the highway.

29

"Where the hell you going?" Leon roared as Roy goosed the little Toyota west on the highway, leaving the cabin behind.

"Away from here!" The rice-burner's engine whined so loudly, they had to shout to be heard. Plus, they had the rattling heater going full blast. Didn't seem to help much; Leon's teeth were chattering. "Didn't you see that fuckin' cop car?"

"I saw it, but we can't just run off!" Leon's voice sounded thick and cloudy in his own ears. His wheezing made him regret every Marlboro he'd ever smoked.

Roy took his foot off the accelerator and the little car sputtered and slowed. "What the hell d'you suggest? You wanta go back there, shoot it out with the cops?"

"Naw, but shit, we can't just leave Junior there."

"Don't know why not," Roy said. "Little fucker's never done us any good."

"He's my brother!"

"I don't give a rat's ass. I ain't going back to jail because Junior can't keep himself out of trouble."

Leon eyed his partner. "You better stop this fuckin' car, Roy. Or you're gonna have more trouble than you can handle."

Roy snorted. "From who? You? You should see your face. You look like something a dog puked up."

Leon clamped his teeth together, but he couldn't hold them that way long. He opened his mouth and sucked air.

"We can't leave Junior. We got him into this and we got to get him out."

"Can't you see it's too late, dammit? That old fucker called the cops. Junior's cuffed and stuffed by now."

Leon started to yell some more, but then caught himself. Something wasn't right back at the cabin. Then it came to him. He said, "I don't think so."

Roy was watching the road, pushing the little car, but Leon's sudden calm got his attention. "The hell you mean?"

"Think about it. If Vince called the cops, he'd just be putting himself behind bars. For robbing that bank."

"Not if he blamed it all on us."

"Well, then, at least temporarily. Until the cops sort it out. You heard that old man. He don't want to spend another day behind bars."

Roy reflected on this for a moment, then shook his head. "Don't matter who called them. They're at that cabin."

Leon reached out and jabbed him in the shoulder with a thick index finger. Roy, tense as usual, jumped.

"One cop car, Roy. Just one. That seem right to you?"

Again the Toyota slowed. "What do you mean?"

"If Vince called the cops, told them about the bank robbery, told them his wife had been held hostage, you think the cops would send just one car?"

"I dunno."

"Hell, no, man, they'd send everything they have. The whole force would be there, lights flashing, sirens going. Be the biggest thing to happen in this shithole in years."

Roy's lower lip stuck out and his brow furrowed.

"Something else is going on at that cabin," Leon said. "Just that one police car. Vince is running a scam on them, trying to get some protection."

"Protection from what?"

"From *us*, numbnuts. He knew we'd come after him, soon as we found ourselves a ride. He probably called the cops, made up some whopper, just to get that car there."

"You think?"

"Sure. We can wait 'em out. If they don't bust Vince, then we still got a chance to get even with him. And to get that loot."

Roy scowled as he steered the little car through another curve. Finally, he said, "You just want to go back there and rescue your dumbshit brother."

"I want that money, too. And I want to make that old man pay for this broken nose."

Roy hit the brakes. A sign pointed to the left, alerting travelers to the Whiskeytown Lake visitors' center. Roy swerved across the oncoming lane, bounced into the parking lot, and pulled the car to a halt. He turned to look dead-on at Leon.

"We'll go back there," Roy said. "Drive past the cabin. But if the cops are still there, I'm gonna keep driving. We're in a stolen car. Cops are looking all over for us. I ain't shooting it out with them. Not for Junior's sake."

Leon's face ached. He ran a hand across his brow, massaged his forehead for a second. Roy still didn't get it. Sometimes, it was like talking to a goddamned mule.

"We can't let the cops take Junior."

"I don't see why not."

"Because he knows everything about *us*," Leon said tightly. "Junior'll talk. You know he will. Little shit couldn't stand up to a meter maid, much less some tough old deputy who knows what he's doin'. He'll tell 'em everything about us and Vince and that bank. Then where will we be?"

Roy made a face. "Fucked."

"That's right. Now turn this shitbird around and let's go get him."

"And if those cops are still there?"

Leon raised his black pistol. "Then some folks gonna die. And it ain't gonna be us."

30

Debra drove toward home, thinking how the Carsons were a likeable old couple. Lots of such people living up here in the woods. Lot of rednecks and hermits and weirdos, too, but it helped to remember that not all who lived out in the sticks were marijuana-growing, gun-toting freaks. In her job, she encountered more of the goobers than the good ones. But the Carsons seemed like fine people.

She still had a funny feeling about that blood on their sidewalk. The whole story about the dog seemed slightly off somehow. And the old man sitting around in rain-soaked trousers, reading. Debra thought she was good at sizing up situations, but this one seemed just beyond her grasp.

Enough. She'd wasted the whole morning on this goose chase. If she went straight to bed, she might get five or six hours' sleep, enough that she wouldn't be a total zombie when her next shift began at 7 p.m. Maybe. If she could sleep.

Out of habit, she glanced at the screen of her on-board computer. The sheriff's office shared the SHASCOM computer system with the Redding Police Department, and she could see the city boys were getting all the action today. A bank robbery in Redding still was the top item on the screen, and she could see from the coded entries that six or seven officers were involved. There'd been a carjacking, too, just a few blocks away from the bank. A carjacking? In Redding? Had to be related to the bank robbery in some way. She wondered how the city detectives were handling both investigations at once, whether they were working the two incidents together, whether the feds had arrived yet.

Just her usual curiosity, not that it mattered. RPD wouldn't ask for help from the sheriff's department, not unless it was absolutely necessary. The two departments had feuded for years over turf and funding and anything else you could name. And, hell, Debra reminded herself, she wasn't officially on duty anyway. As far as anyone at the office knew, she was home sleeping, which is exactly where she should be.

Another line of green code popped up on the computer screen. Public disturbance, no big deal. Then the address registered with Debra. Shasta Liquors.

"Oh, hell," she said aloud. "What have Coral and Pearl done now?"

Without even thinking about it, she braked and flipped on her flashers. Swung the car through a U-turn and zoomed west, past the Carsons' cabin, toward the tiny burg of Shasta.

31

Vince opened the bedroom door and looked in at Junior. The boy lay on his side, twisting against the duct tape, his face turning blue. Bubbles of blood burbled from his nostrils. Vince squatted beside him and yanked the duct tape off his mouth. Junior gasped loudly.

"Good thing that deputy didn't stick around longer," Vince said to Maria, who watched anxiously from the doorway. "Junior might not have made it."

"I *told* you his nose was broken," she said.

"Chance I had to take. What if he'd started howling while she was here?"

On cue, Junior moaned and mumbled something. Vince poked his chest with a stiff finger. "You need to keep quiet, unless you want me to put that tape back."

Junior shook his head. Breathing had become important to him.

"What do we do now?" Maria asked, a tremor in her voice.

"Same as before. Get ready for those other idiots to show up."

He got to his feet, then bent over and grabbed the collar of Junior's blood-dappled shirt. Walking backward, he dragged Junior into the kitchen. The boy slid along easily on the hard-wood floor.

Vince paused in the kitchen while Maria moved the throw rug

out of the way. She looked at the bloodstains on the underside of the rug.

"Damn," she said. "This is ruined."

"That was quick thinking on your part, covering up that blood." Vince dragged Junior through the archway. "That deputy might've believed I carried a bloody dog up to the porch, but there wouldn't have been any reason to take it into the kitchen."

Maria rolled up the rug and stuck it in the kitchen trash can. "You think she believed us?"

"She went away, and that's all I was after."

He straightened up and put both hands on his lower back. His muscles were already taut, and all the stooping was giving him a backache.

"You know," he said, "I think I saw that deputy earlier today. We passed a patrol car as we were driving into town. Looked like the same woman. Isn't that the damnedest thing?"

"I'm not surprised," Maria said. "Seems like she's stopping by every twenty minutes."

Vince bent over with a groan and grabbed Junior's collar again. He dragged him the length of the living room, the duct-taped kid sliding along the floor like a mummy. Maria hurried past, moving chairs and rugs out of the way.

Just inside the front door, he stopped and let go of Junior's collar. The kid's turbaned head thunked onto the floor.

"This'll do," Vince said. "Where'd you hide the guns?"

"They're in the kitchen."

He followed Maria back to the kitchen, to the little pantry that filled one corner. The pantry wasn't much bigger than a closet, with shelves full of canned goods along one wall and a clothes washer and dryer against the other. Vince's revolvers sat on a shelf next to the two zippered bank bags.

"Good thing that deputy didn't want to search the place," she said. "One look in here would've changed everything."

"No cause for a search," Vince said. "She suspected something was up, though. I could see it in her eyes."

He tucked the bank bags behind some canned goods, and picked up the pistols.

"Think she'll be back?" Maria asked.

"Hope not. Be hard to explain Junior. And I don't feel up to dragging him all the way back to the bedroom again."

Concern creased Maria's face. Vince grinned at her.

"I'm fine," he said before she could ask. "Probably good for me to get some exercise."

She shook her head, fighting back a smile. "You're crazy, you know that?"

She moved close to him, pressed against his chest, hugging him tight. He had a pistol in either hand, but he wrapped his arms around her and squeezed.

After a few seconds, she sighed and let him loose, and he handed her one of the guns. He made sure the back door was locked and deadbolted, and they went to the living room. Junior still lay just inside the front door, squirming.

"Okay," Maria said. "Where do you want me?"

Several answers flitted through his mind: Somewhere safe. Somewhere far away from the cabin. Maybe hiding in the woods or sitting behind the wheel of the Plymouth, ready to race away. But he knew she wouldn't leave his side. He just prayed she wouldn't be hurt.

"Over there," he said. "We'll watch out the windows."

"And when they show up?"

"Maybe they won't."

Maria frowned. "They'll come. Leon won't leave his little brother."

Vince tried smiling at her, but he knew the expression looked forced. It *felt* forced.

"A brother's love," he said. "I'm counting on that."

Junior groaned.

32

The scene Deputy Debra Kemp found at Shasta Liquors wasn't much different from what she'd seen the night before. Broken glass and spilled booze and blood everywhere.

This time, though, the blood belonged to the two old sisters who ran the place. And there was another witness, Flora Hardaway, an orange-haired matron who belonged to every civic group in Shasta County as well as the same Methodist church Debra had attended since she was a child.

Wearing a lavender pantsuit, Mrs. Hardaway was waiting just inside the door when Debra barreled through.

"I saw the whole thing," she declared. "Coral started it."

"Shut up, you bitch!" Coral shrieked. She didn't take her eyes off her sister, though. The Bingham sisters were on opposite sides of the store, glaring at each other. Both were dressed in the same sort of loose clothes they'd worn the night before, though Coral's sleeve was torn at the shoulder. She had a wine bottle in her hand, waving it menacingly. Blood trickled from her nose. Pearl had a split lip and her long gray hair was tousled, looked like someone had been yanking it out by the handful.

"What the hell is going on here?" Debra bellowed.

That got the sisters' attention. Pearl ducked her head and fingered her bloody mouth. Coral tucked the wine bottle behind her hefty hip, as if she could hide it now.

"They were showing me that video," Mrs. Hardaway twittered. "The one of the robbery?"

Debra glanced up, saw the videotape was freeze-framed at the moment when the bloodied robber fled out the door.

"I told them I didn't care to see it." Mrs. Hardaway's eyes were round behind her gold-rimmed eyeglasses. She held a cell phone in one hand and clutched her big handbag to her chest with the other. "There's enough of that sort of thing on regular TV."

"Uh-huh." Debra felt stupid. No sleep, a full morning of confusion, her theories shot all to hell. Now this.

"I just stopped by here for some cooking sherry," Mrs. Hardaway said. "You know I don't approve of liquor. But some recipes call for—"

"Just tell me what happened."

"Well, Pearl said she guessed she was the real hero, since she was the first one to take a crack at that boy. And Coral said she was, you know, full of it. Well, Pearl didn't like that. She said something ugly—I won't repeat it—and Coral just slapped her right in the face!"

Debra looked to the sisters. They both played contrite now, staring at the floor. Despite the gray hair and the flab and the wrinkles, they reminded her of two little girls who'd been caught doing something naughty.

"Next thing I know," Mrs. Hardaway said, "they were going at it. Slapping and punching and pulling hair and throwing bottles. I've never seen anything like it, two grown women acting that way. *I* wasn't about to get in the middle of it. I whipped out my phone and dialed 911."

Debra sighed heavily. This she did not need.

"I must say," Mrs. Hardaway concluded, "you certainly got here fast."

"I was nearby."

"Sure, *now* you get here in a hurry," Pearl said. "Where were you last night, when we were getting robbed?"

Debra rolled her eyes. She heard a car bump into the parking lot, and flashers threw red light through the glass door. Thank God. She peered out the glass door, saw Deputy Bill Murphy unfolding from his cruiser. She liked Murphy. A good deputy. Handsome, too. She'd always put him in the category of too-bad-he's-happily-married. It was a well-populated category.

"I'm not even on duty," she said. "But here's an officer from the day shift. He'll get this straightened out."

Murphy came inside, looking around warily.

"What are you doing here?" he asked Debra.

"Just passing through," she said. "This is all yours."

Murphy frowned, looked like he didn't want any part of whatever had occurred in the liquor store.

Debra pointed at each of the Binghams, wielding her finger like a gun. "I want to say, though, that you two should be ashamed of yourselves. You're sisters! You've worked together all your lives and now this? Both of you so proud of outsmarting that robber that you end up wailing away on each other?"

The sisters muttered and shuffled their feet.

"If I wasn't so tired, I'd take you to jail myself," she said. "But I'll leave it to Deputy Murphy here to make that decision."

"I think you ought to arrest them both," Mrs. Hardaway proclaimed.

"Shut up!" both sisters shouted at her.

"Well, I never—"

"Yes, shut up," Debra said. "You better hope Deputy Murphy can settle this without anyone pressing charges. Otherwise, you'll get to testify in court about what you were doing at a liquor store."

Mrs. Hardaway blinked rapidly. Her mouth hung open.

"Cooking sherry, my ass," Debra said.

She headed for the door, slapping Murphy on the shoulder as she passed.

"They're all yours, Bill."

Murphy looked as if he'd like to run right out the door with her.

Outside, Debra climbed behind the wheel of her patrol car, shaking her head and mumbling. "Heroes. For shit's sake."

33

The stolen Toyota sputtered and coughed as it neared the Carsons' driveway. Leon paid no attention, too busy leaning forward, trying to see between the trees to the cabin. The sheriff's department car was gone.

"See, what did I tell you?" he said. "I'll bet it was one of those cop cars we saw back at that liquor store. They're already onto something else. Now we got that old bastard right where we want him."

Roy spun the steering wheel, and the little car jounced through mud puddles between the pines. It coughed again and died, rolling silently forward, halfway across the clearing in front of the cabin before coming to a halt.

Roy leaned forward, studying the lights and gauges on the dashboard. "Damn."

"What?"

"Ran out of gas."

"Shit, that don't matter none," Leon said brightly. "My car's still out back. We finish our business here, and we'll ride away in style."

Roy pumped the accelerator and cranked the ignition. The starter whined, but the engine refused to catch.

"Leave it. We don't need this car."

Roy cranked it again, muttering curses. Goddamn, the boy was hard-headed.

"It's a good thing, leaving this car here," Leon said. "Cops find it, and it'll make 'em wonder. They'll think whoever boosted the car were the same ones who killed Vince and his wife."

Roy paused, then looked over at him, scowling. "It *will be* the same ones. Us."

"Yeah, but *they* don't know that."

Roy's brow furrowed as he tried to sort that out.

"Let's just go," Leon said. "Get this done."

They checked their pistols, then popped open the little car's tinny doors. Leon kept his eyes on the cabin's curtained windows as they unfolded from the Toyota.

"I don't see that Plymouth nowhere," Roy said. "Think he ran off?"

"Nah, he wouldn't leave his wife behind."

"Maybe he came and got her. Maybe they ran off together."

"Then what were the cops doing here?"

Roy shook his head. He looked stunned and confused.

"Vince is around here somewhere," Leon said. "Bet on it. He's probably got Junior in the house."

"Maybe he killed Junior."

"Damn, Roy, don't say that! If Junior's dead, I'll never hear the end of it."

They still stood by the car, neither in any hurry to rush the cabin. Leon heard a latch click, and he and Roy crouched behind the car doors, pointing their pistols at the cabin.

The front door swung inward, opening slowly.

Leon squinted, trying to see through the door into the cabin's dim interior. Looked like a bundle of some kind on the floor, three or four feet inside the door. Rags maybe, white and blue and gray. Then the bundle moved, and he recognized it as Junior, lying on his face, his hands bound behind him with duct tape.

"Goddamn!" Leon said. "Junior?"

Then something else came into view through the open door—a gray-sleeved arm reaching forward, near the floor, the hand holding a pistol. Vince stayed out of sight behind the door, just his arm sticking out, the barrel of the pistol resting against Junior's turbaned head.

"Shit!" Leon yelled. "Hold on there, Vince!"

Vince peered around the door with one eye, his snowy head barely exposed, his squatting body protected by the thick wooden door.

Leon heard the hammer click back on Roy's revolver. "Wait, Roy. You don't have a clean shot."

He glanced over, saw that Roy had one eye closed, aiming.

"Don't. Even if you hit him, his finger'll jerk and he'll blow Junior's head off."

The old man had said nothing so far, but he'd apparently been listening. "You tell him, Leon," he shouted. "This gun's got a hair trigger."

Leon saw the curtains move in one of the front windows, the one on the right, in back of Vince. He noticed that the window was open a few inches. The barrel of a pistol jutted out above the sill. The old woman, hiding behind the curtain. Must be kneeling down, aiming, using the windowsill to hold her hand steady. Shit. Looked steady as a rock to him. He couldn't imagine that kindly old nurse shooting somebody, but he'd rather not find out.

Roy saw it, too. He shifted his gun back and forth, trying to cover both the Carsons. He and Leon crouched lower behind the car doors. Leon thinking: These doors are awfully thin. Would they even stop a bullet?

"Looks like we got a standoff," he shouted.

"That's right," Vince yelled back. "You boys take it easy. All I want to do is talk."

They exchanged a glance through the open car. Roy's face had darkened with rage. Leon didn't like the looks of that. Once he got a mad going, there was no stopping him.

"Be cool, Roy. Let's hear what the man has to say."

Roy kept his gun aimed at the cabin. Leon thinking: Damn, somebody's got to set the ball rolling here. He stood up and let his pistol dangle at his side. The center of his chest ached, as if he could feel a bullet headed his way. But he held his position, for Junior's sake.

"All right, Vince," he shouted. "Let's hear it."

The old man peered around the door.

"I don't want to kill your brother," he called. "But I'll do it if I have to."

Leon heard another noise, sounded like a whimper from Junior. The kid lay perfectly still.

"I just want this all to be over," Vince said.

"Sure, dad, that's all we want, too. No reason for anybody to get killed here."

Roy growled low in his throat, irritated and impatient.

"Here's my proposition," Vince said. "You boys throw your guns away—"

Roy snorted.

"—and I'll hand over Junior. Then you get in your car and get the hell out of here."

That didn't sound like much of a deal to Leon. They toss their guns, and Vince could come right out that door, blasting away. One thing for Junior to get shot, but it was another for Leon to take a bullet himself.

He bent his knees, ready to drop back down behind the car door.

"No deal," he shouted. "Shoot Junior if you have to, but we want that loot. We're not leaving here without it."

"You think you can come in here and get it?"

"If we have to, it ain't gonna be pretty."

Nothing from Vince for several seconds.

"All right," he said finally. "Throw away your guns and you get Junior *and* the money. But then you've got to leave and never come back. So far, the cops don't seem to be onto us for the bank robbery. I'd like to keep it that way."

"Who you kidding, dad? We already saw that cop car here. You cut a deal with them? Get us disarmed, so they can wait for us up the road?"

Vince shook his head. He'd leaned a little farther forward. Just a little more, and Roy would have a shot at him.

"That deputy knows nothing about the bank," Vince said. "She was here for something else."

"Yeah? And what would that be?"

"She saw the blood Junior dripped all over the sidewalk last night. We told her I'd hit a dog with a car and that was what left the blood."

Leon considered that. Sounded like quick thinking, coming up with such a story. What would he have done, put in the same position? Hell, he probably would've just let Roy shoot the deputy.

"She might come back," Vince said. "It would be better if we get this resolved."

Leon said nothing, making him wait.

"You get Junior and the loot," the old man said. "We get left alone."

Leon glanced over at Roy, saw that his hotheaded partner still drew down on Vince, ready to fire. His cheek twitched, but his hands were steady.

"Throw aside those weapons," Vince ordered.

"Fuck that!" Roy yelled, and he pulled the trigger.

The revolver roared and spat fire. A chunk of wood splintered away from the thick door as Vince jerked back out of sight.

Leon fell to his knees behind the car door, bringing up his gun. The cabin door slammed shut.

Another pistol cracked, and Roy said, "Unnh!"

Leon looked over, saw blood spritzing from Roy's meaty right shoulder. Didn't make Roy hesitate, though. He blasted away at the cabin, blowing glass out of both front windows and knocking splinters out of the front door.

"Stop it, Roy! Stop!"

But he didn't stop until he ran out of bullets. Then he crouched lower beside the car, began fishing in the chest pocket of his jean jacket for more ammo.

"Goddamn it, Roy! What about Junior?"

Roy looked through the open car at Leon. His face was red and shiny, and his eyes looked wild.

"Fuck him," he said. "He's a dead man."

"Maybe it's not too late. We can—"

"It is so too late," Roy said. "I'm killing 'em. You with me or not?"

Roy's thick fingers shoved cartridges into the chambers of the pistol. He looked crazy-mad. Leon knew better than to disagree with him now.

"Sure, Roy. Let's go get 'em."

34

Vince crouched beside the closed door as bullets thudded into the thick walls and ricocheted through the shattered windows. The thunder of the gunfire echoed through the forest. He wondered how far the noise would carry, how much time he had.

"My God, Vince," Maria cried. "I shot that man!"

She was prone on the floor under the window, shards of glass sparkling on the back of her white blouse and in her silver hair. The curtains above her were shredded. Her face was flushed and her eyes were round and filling with tears, but he couldn't take time to comfort her. Not now.

"Stay down," he said. "They'll be coming."

He crawled on his stomach past Junior, then turned around and used his feet to push Junior nearer the door. The immobilized idiot would make a good doorstop.

He crawled over to the other window. Maybe he could draw their fire to that side, keep Maria safe for the moment.

He peeked around the splintered window frame, saw Roy and Leon crouched on either side of the little blue car, behind the doors. Leon watched the house, his pistol pointed toward the porch, his wet black hair dripping into his face. Roy appeared to be reloading. They were talking, but Vince couldn't make out the words.

If only these fools would've listened to reason. If only they'd taken their money and Junior and gone. Vince didn't want to shoot it out with them, and he sure as hell didn't like jeopardizing Maria's safety. But it was too late to turn back now. Someone would've heard the shots, called the cops. Vince was looking at prison again, no question, soon as the cops sorted out his real identity. Damn it.

Anger filling him, he snaked his pistol through the broken window and fired twice at Roy. The bullets punched holes in the car door, but Vince couldn't tell whether they'd pierced through to the other side. Roy fell flat in the mud.

Vince ducked back as Leon fired. Bullets whined through the window and shattered something on the far wall. He didn't turn to look.

His ears ringing, Vince chanced another peek outside, saw Leon charging toward the cabin. Roy fired another fusillade at the window, and Vince flinched back out of the way.

He leapt up as Leon's boots thumped onto the wooden porch. Maria still lay beneath the far window, her feet scrabbling against the floor, like she was trying to get up to greet Leon with her gun. Vince gestured for her to stay put, and pointed his pistol at the door.

The doorknob turned, and Leon tried to throw it open. But the door hit his inert brother and stopped just as he tried to plunge inside. Junior howled. Leon's battered face smacked against the half-open door. He howled, too.

Vince reached his pistol through the gap and planted the steel barrel against Leon's bearded cheek.

"Shit!" Leon's voice seemed suddenly higher.

"You'd better hold real still. I shoot, and they'll never find all the pieces of your head."

Vince reached through the opening with his free hand and grabbed Leon's pistol. Wrested it from his grip and tossed it to the floor behind him. He tried to see past his captive, see what Roy was doing, but Leon's wide body blocked the way.

"Hold on now, dad."

Vince jabbed his face with the gun. "Stop calling me 'dad.'"

"Okay, okay."

"I was *your* dad, I would've drowned you in a river when you were a kitten. Saved the world a lot of grief."

"Sure. Okay." All of Leon's attention was on the pistol that stabbed at his face.

Vince heard movement outside, probably Roy running toward the cabin, ready to fly through one of the broken windows like Superman. That boy was insane.

"Tell your buddy to throw down his gun."

"Sure, daa—" He caught himself in time. "Roy!"

No answer. Leon's face squinched up in puzzlement.

"Roy?"

35

The deputy heard the gunshots from the highway. Hard to miss them, booming around the forested hills. Debra braked her cruiser, recognized that she was near the driveway to the Carsons' cabin. Oh, my Lord, she thought. Now what?

The shooting stopped as she swung the car off the highway, between the pine trees. As it bumped onto the muddy drive, she fumbled with her radio, calling for backup, reporting "shots fired." Got an immediate answer from the dispatcher. A thought flashed through Debra's mind: Bill Murphy wasn't far away, back at the liquor store. He could be here in minutes.

Debra heard the dispatcher relaying an all-points as the cruiser crept forward. A blue Toyota sat in the clearing, halfway to the house, both doors standing open. The windows of the cabin were shattered and the walls looked pocked by bullets. A big, hairy, soaking-wet man was at the front door. Another bruiser, this one with a Mohawk and bright red blood on his sopping denim jacket, was between the Toyota and the porch. He was turning her way, and he had a pistol in his hand.

Debra hit her siren, one long whoop that froze the man in place for a second. Then he leveled the revolver at her. She stomped the brakes and fell sideways in the seat, her on-board computer and other gear jabbing her ribs, just as the windshield loudly shattered.

She threw the car into Park, then yanked the handle on the car door and slithered out as it swung open. Squatting behind the door, she pulled her Glock from her holster and brought it up as the shooter turned to run. She braced her wrist in perfect position and fired twice, but he dodged around the corner of the cabin. She'd missed him.

She swung the other way, ready to shoot the man on the porch. But he was already falling, his feet kicked out from under him. He landed heavily on his back as Vince Carson sprang through the doorway, a pistol in his hand. The old man landed on the big guy's chest, jammed the gun into his face.

"Freeze!" she shouted.

Carson looked up at her, his white hair wild, his eyes narrow and fierce.

"I said freeze!"

He straightened up, still straddling the other man's broad chest. He lifted the gun, pointing it away from Debra, then let it go loose in his hand. It dangled on his finger by the trigger guard.

Debra looked all around for the one who'd run off. She couldn't see him anywhere, and that made her uneasy. He could be behind any one of those trees, waiting to unload on her as soon as she moved.

Her hands were shaking, her gun pointed at the porch. Vince Carson sat still, the way she'd left him. The big guy put one hand up and covered his face with it, but otherwise didn't twitch.

"Throw that gun out into the yard," she shouted to Carson. "Then get off him."

The old man did as he was told. After he tossed the gun, he crawled a few feet away from the downed man and sat on his knees, his heels up under his buttocks. He smoothed his white hair back away from his face, seemed to be calming down.

"Just stay where you are," she shouted. "Help's on the way."

Debra stayed behind the protective covering of the open

car door. She needed to move, to get the men on the porch lying face down, put the cuffs on them. It would look better if she had them fully in custody when the other deputies arrived. But she worried about the one who was still loose. Should she risk a dash up to the porch?

The maroon curtains moved behind one of the shattered windows. Debra shifted her aim toward the movement, then saw Mrs. Carson's silvery head poke between the tattered curtains. She appeared to be kneeling inside the window. She smiled and waved. Debra couldn't help herself—she smiled back.

"Boy," Mrs. Carson shouted, "are we glad to see you!"

36

Maria didn't like the idea of going outside the safe walls of the cabin, not with Roy still on the loose out there, wounded and infuriated. But Deputy Kemp ordered her to come outside, and she moved to obey, ducking out from under the curtains and shakily getting to her feet. Shards of glass shattered to the floor around her. She carefully shook her blouse, and more glass fell.

Junior still lay nearby, moaning. The shattered glass hadn't reached him, but she figured he'd been hurt plenty by the swinging door.

She still held her warm pistol, and recognized she shouldn't carry it outside. The deputy could get the wrong idea. Maria bent and slid the gun across the hardwood floor. It went under the sofa, out of sight. Not what she intended, but just as well.

Glass crunching under her shoes, she stepped around Junior, then slipped out the partly open door. She pulled it closed behind her. She didn't think the young deputy had seen Junior trussed up inside, and she was in no hurry to show her. The situation was confused enough already.

Vince still knelt near Leon, and Maria went to the other side of her husband, keeping away from the fallen man. Deputy Kemp yelled for them all to lie face down on the porch. Leon grunted as he rolled over on his stomach. Vince nodded to Maria, letting her know it was fine. He lay down on the wooden floor and she knelt beside him, her knees popping, then stretched out flat.

Maria heard a siren in the distance. The sound hit Deputy Kemp like a starter's pistol; she suddenly sprinted up the flagstone sidewalk and up the steps onto the porch. She kept glancing around at the surrounding forest, searching for Roy.

The deputy circled to her right, her pistol trained on the three of them. Maria noticed her heavy black boots, which were at eye level now. How could a woman go around in shoes like that?

Leon groaned and turned his head toward the deputy. She looked down at him, her gun still extended in both hands, her finger outside the trigger guard. Her eyes widened when she saw the blood on Leon's battered face, the broken nose that veered off to one side.

"My God," she said, "what happened to you?"

"That old man hit me."

Vince twisted his neck to look up at the deputy. Maria couldn't see his face, just the back of his head. She heard him say, a warning in his tone, "He's not—"

Too late. Leon pushed up from the floor. Scrabbling with his hands and knees, he threw himself sideways at the deputy. His broad torso hit her in the knees, and she stumbled backward and lost her balance.

She unleashed one little yelp, then hit hard on her back, and Maria felt the wooden floor vibrate from the impact. The deputy's black pistol went flying. It skittered across the wooden porch, all the way to the edge above the front steps.

Leon dived at the deputy and scrambled to get on top of her, trying to pin her down. Maria heard a scream and realized it was coming from her own mouth.

Vince crawled forward on elbows and knees, going for the pistol, which was dangerously close to Leon. Maria shouted his name, but he didn't seem to hear.

Leon could've lunged and beaten Vince to the gun, but he was busy with the deputy. He was on top of her now, straddling her abdomen, swinging his big fists. She fought back, grunting and slugging and kicking. From Maria's vantage point, they looked like a squirming snakes' nest of fists and boots and knees.

Vince sprang to his feet, the gun in his hand. He whirled and cracked Leon just above the ear with the barrel of the pistol. Leon's head snapped to the side. He stopped fighting the deputy. Seemed to teeter for a second, then fell sideways. Maria couldn't tell whether he was unconscious, but he stopped moving, and that was good enough for now.

Deputy Kemp kicked her legs, getting untangled, then sat up, her eyes wide, her square face red from exertion and Leon's blows. She went very still when she saw Vince standing over her, the pistol in his hand.

The siren was closer now, and he cocked his head at the sound. Maria didn't take her eyes off him. She sent him mental signals, *willing* him to hand over the gun and surrender.

Vince glanced over his shoulder and smiled at her. He spun the gun around in his hand so that it no longer pointed toward the deputy. He bent at the waist and handed the pistol to Deputy Kemp. Her hands shook as she reached up and took it.

He stretched a hand out to the deputy. "Want me to help you up? Or should I just lie back down?"

The deputy took Vince's hand, let him hoist her to her feet. She looked shaken and flushed, but she managed a sheepish grin.

Brakes shrieked on the pavement at the end of the driveway, then a squad car burst through the trees, its red lights flashing, and pulled up short behind the deputy's car in a sliding growl of gravel. A lanky young man, dressed in sheriff's department khaki-and-olive drab, leaped out, a shotgun in his hands.

"It's okay, Bill," Deputy Kemp shouted. "But watch the trees. There's another one out there somewhere. He's armed."

The tall deputy did as he was told, sticking close to his car, surveying the forest, the shotgun at his shoulder. More sirens wailed in the distance.

Leon groaned and shifted on the floor. Deputy Kemp pointed her pistol at him while she got handcuffs off her belt. She gestured with the pistol for Vince to back up, and he did. Then she squatted beside Leon and expertly cuffed his hands behind his back, her movements quick and efficient.

Maria wondered whether she'd cuff Vince next. She knew her husband wouldn't like that. But the deputy stood up and took a ragged breath, scanning the forest once more before turning her attention to Vince.

"Now," she said, "you want to tell me what the hell is going on here?"

37

Behind the closed door, Junior Daggett felt his heart pounding against the hardwood floor. Leon's black pistol was only a couple of feet from his head, where Vince had tossed it. If only he could get loose and reach it ...

He knew he was kidding himself. First of all, there was no getting free from the duct tape. Maria had done a good job of binding him. Secondly, he'd heard the sirens outside. Even if he was loose, the gun in his hands, he'd never have the guts to go up against the Law.

He could hear Vince talking in low tones to a woman, and Junior guessed it was the deputy who'd been at the house earlier. He'd heard all the scuffling and wrestling on the porch, but it had been several minutes since he heard Leon's voice. Things sounded pretty calm now, which meant Leon was somehow out of the picture. Cuffed? Out cold? Dead? Junior's stomach flopped at the thought.

And where the hell was Roy? Mr. Tough Guy, always bragging about how well he handled himself when the shit hit the fan, where was he now? Roy had been the one to start the shooting, no regard for Junior's safety, but now he seemed to have disappeared. At least, Junior couldn't hear him anywhere. And if Roy Wade was still out there, you could bet there'd be gunfire. Maybe he was dead, too.

Junior grimaced, which made his smashed nose hurt so bad, his eyes filled with tears. Goddamned Roy Wade. Goddamned Leon. He wished he'd never come along on their "crime spree."

The three of them were good and truly fucked. The old bank robber and his wife had outwitted them at every turn, and now the law was here, ready to haul them away. The shooting had scared Junior half to death, the bullets whining and the shattered glass flying all around him. But even worse was the realization now that he was going to jail, a place filled with homicidal brutes like Roy Wade. The thought was nearly more than he could bear.

Junior caught himself whimpering. He clamped his mouth shut, but that didn't work long. He needed it open to breathe. His nose was swollen shut and his face still throbbed, and the dull ache deep in his shoulder, where the door hit it when Leon tried to charge into the cabin, made him think it might be broken.

The deputy and Vince still talked out on the porch. Maria spoke occasionally, too, but Junior was too upset to focus on what they were saying. He gasped heavily, trying to pull more air into his lungs, trying to keep from sobbing.

Then the front door clicked open and he heard Vince say, "There's something else we should show you."

Junior tried to roll out of the way; he didn't need another whap on that shoulder. But the door opened gently this time, barely touched him. Vince stepped through the narrow opening, then grabbed Junior's collar and dragged him away from the door.

The fat-assed deputy stepped into the doorway, a pistol in her hand. A strand of dark hair had come loose from her ponytail and hung down over one eye. Her square-jawed face was splotchy and red.

"I'll be damned," she muttered when she saw Junior on the floor.

Now, he thought. Now's when I need to say something, turn the tide here, try to shift the blame. Get her after Vince rather than me and Leon. But he couldn't summon up the words. The sight of her uniform and her badge and that gun sucked all the wind out of him, made his mind go blank. He was going to jail now. That much was certain. And life as he knew it would never be the same.

"This is the brother of that mutt you cuffed outside," Vince said. "They call him Junior."

38

Vince dragged Junior out onto the porch for the deputy, lined him up beside his groaning brother. Then he noticed Maria, standing now, over against the wall of the cabin, keeping a wary eye on the trees in the direction where Roy had disappeared.

He went to her, wrapped his arms around her. She took a deep, trembling breath and relaxed against him. He thought she might be weeping, but he didn't lean back to check. He wanted to be in close, his mouth right beside her ear.

"It's okay, hon," he whispered. "Just follow my lead."

He felt her nod against his shoulder.

"Leave the talking to me," he said. "If they separate us, say you're too upset to answer questions."

Another nod.

He sensed the young deputy hovering behind him. He straightened and raised a hand to stroke his wife's hair, keeping her close in case he got a chance to tell her more.

Another squad car screamed to a halt on the highway. Vince looked through the trees, counted five total. Every Sheriff's Department vehicle on duty in the county, he guessed, right here at my cabin. We're in it deep now.

An older officer came marching up the driveway. He was slightly built and balding, and wore a thick brown mustache that curved around the corners of his downturned mouth.

"There he is," Deputy Kemp said, sounding relieved. "Good to see you, Lieutenant."

The lieutenant—the name tag on his chest said "Jones"—cocked one eyebrow and glanced around the clearing at his deputies prowling the trees. Then his eyes roamed the porch—Leon and Junior prone on the deck, Maria and Vince in each other's arms, Deputy Kemp with her left eye swelling shut and a bruise arising on her cheekbone.

"The hell's going on here?"

"It's a mess," Deputy Kemp said. "I don't have it all sorted out yet. But apparently that guy"—she pointed at Leon—"is one of the men who did that carjacking in Redding today. His partner ran off in the woods. We're looking for him."

Jones nibbled at his mustache. "Was he armed?"

"Yes, sir," she said. "Shot the windshield out of my cruiser."

He glanced back over his shoulder at the wounded patrol car. Then he shouted, "You men! Pull back! Stay close to the house until we get some more people here."

He turned away, toward the cars, and muttered instructions into a radio microphone pinned to the collar of his khaki shirt. Vince missed most of what he was saying, though he did pick up the words, "SWAT team."

When the lieutenant turned back to them, he asked Kemp, "Did you fire your weapon?"

"Yes, sir. But I missed him."

He nodded, didn't seem surprised. He looked again toward the bullet-pocked cars. "That's the Toyota that got jacked?"

"That's what Murphy says. He ran the plates. When I rolled up here, it was sitting just like that, with the doors open, and the carjackers were attacking this cabin."

The lieutenant's eyebrows crawled up his high forehead.

"What were they doing *here*?" he asked. "And who are these other people?"

"That one," she said, pointing at Junior, "is this one's brother. Apparently an accomplice."

Junior groaned, but didn't object to the characterization.

"And these folks are Mr. and Mrs. Carson. They live here."

"What about you?" Jones said to Kemp. "You're not even on duty, are you?"

The lieutenant finally seemed to have noticed the deputy's swelling cheek. Before she could answer, he said, "What happened to your face?"

She took a deep breath. "It's a long story."

Junior moaned again, getting Jones' attention. Four deputies had filtered out of the trees and were gathering near the porch. The lieutenant held up a finger to stop Kemp before she could go on, and spoke to the other officers. "Get those two and lock them in separate cruisers. I'll hear from them in a minute."

Two deputies thumped up onto the porch and grabbed Leon and pulled him to his feet. The other two hesitated, looking puzzled about how to handle Junior. Then they shrugged at each other and bent over and hoisted him up and carried him off to the waiting cars like a rolled-up carpet.

Jones sighed and massaged his forehead, as if he were trying to rub away a sudden headache.

"Lieutenant?" Vince ventured. "If I may speak? I might be able to shed a little light on this situation."

"You'll get your chance in a minute," he said. "But we need to get this area secured first. Kemp?"

"Yes, sir?"

"Take these folks into the living room while I get things organized. We don't need them standing around out here on the porch. What if the one who's loose starts shooting?"

Vince had been thinking the same thing.

"We'll take them downtown in a few minutes, do the interviews there," he said. "You can ride with me."

Vince went inside, his arms still around Maria, thinking he might get an opportunity to whisper more instructions to her. But Deputy Kemp was right behind them, holstering her gun as she went through the cabin door.

Leon's gun still lay on the floor where he'd tossed it earlier, and Vince steered Maria away from it. He wondered what had happened to the gun Maria fired, but this wasn't the time to ask.

The deputy said, "Someone will be in here in a minute to bag that gun. It's evidence now."

Vince wondered whether the cops would search the whole house, whether they'd find the money bags where he'd stashed them in the pantry, or the wig in the closet. If they did, that was the end. No amount of explaining would keep him out of prison.

Nothing he could do about it, though. He needed to act as if it was all over now, as if he were relieved to have been rescued by the cops.

Vince thinking: Leon and Junior ought to be the ones who're relieved. The cops saved those bastards from me.

39

Maria still felt shaky as Deputy Kemp and Lieutenant Jones marched them to one of the squad cars ten minutes later. She'd put on a green coat of heavy wool, but still felt chilled. Vince, wearing his bright yellow windbreaker, kept her tight to his side, his arm around her shoulders. She kept glancing at the dim forest, wondering about Roy.

They passed the police cars where Junior and Leon were stashed. Junior sat staring into his own lap, as if his neck had collapsed under the weight of his turban of bandages. Leon glared at them, his nose pushed over to one side of his bearded face. He looked like a painting by Picasso.

Maria heard brakes squeal, and she looked up to see a large black van, the size of a bread truck, pulling to a stop out on the highway. Its rear doors flew open, and men spilled out. They carried rifles and shotguns and they wore bullet-proof vests and helmets and big black boots. Maria's breath caught in her throat at the sight of them.

"Here's the search team," Deputy Kemp said beside her. "If anybody can find that other carjacker, it's them."

Jones took a minute to talk to the team leader. Maria turned away as Deputy Kemp opened the back door of a squad car for her and Vince.

"Watch your heads," the deputy said automatically.

Maria slid across the hard plastic seat, making room for Vince.

As soon as Deputy Kemp closed the door, Vince was talking, his eyes focused straight ahead, his lips barely moving.

"You're doing fine, hon," he muttered. "Keep acting like you're in shock."

"Who's *acting*?"

He smiled tightly.

"We just need to get through the next few hours," he said. "Once they've heard our story, maybe they won't have any reason to check our identities or search the cabin. Remember: they're after Leon and Roy, not us. As far as they know we didn't do anyth—"

Deputy Kemp popped open the front door and slid into the passenger seat. She turned to look over her shoulder at them, through the grillework that separated front from back in the cruiser.

"Sorry about the cage," she said. "But that's where you have to ride. Regulations."

"Don't worry about it, dear," Maria said. "I'll pretend we're in a taxi."

That made the deputy smile.

"It won't take long. We're not going all the way to Anderson, where I work. Lieutenant Jones said we're going to the sheriff's office downtown. They've got a couple of rooms there where we can do the interviews."

"What about Leon and Junior?" Vince asked.

"Probably straight to the jail," she said. "We can interview them there. And they'll need medical attention. They can get that there, too."

"You could use some yourself," Maria said. "You're going to have a black eye. You should be putting ice on that cheek."

Deputy Kemp smiled again. "Soon."

Then Lieutenant Jones climbed in behind the wheel and cranked the engine and they all rode silently as he raced toward Redding, the car's red lights flashing traffic out of their way.

40

Vince kept Maria close beside him as they entered the Shasta County Sheriff's Department office on Court Street. The small office was across from the courthouse, a couple of blocks from the county jail. Too conveniently close for Vince's comfort.

Their feet slapped against the grimy tile floor as they marched down a narrow hallway to a small windowless room in the back of the building. Looked like a file room, with cabinets along two beige walls and curling wanted posters tacked to a bulletin board. A rectangular metal table squatted in the center, surrounded by scoop-style orange plastic chairs, and there was a coffee pot on a counter nearby. Vince guessed the cops used the place for a break room.

Jones gestured him and Maria into chairs, Maria still clinging, acting scared and uncomfortable. Vince figured she'd been in worse places than this during all those years of working at prisons, but he was glad she was playing it this way. He wanted the cops to believe he and Maria were just a couple of frightened senior citizens, not at all savvy to the System.

Seemed to be working, too. They were in this relaxed room rather than an interrogation booth with hidden microphones and video cameras and two-way mirrors. Looked as if they were going to question him and Maria together rather than separately, which would be just the kind of small-town mistake that could salvage this situation. Vince needed Maria to hear his version of events, and it looked like the Shasta County Sheriff's Department would accommodate him.

Kemp and Jones sat in chairs across the table from them, and everyone shucked their jackets. It was warm in the small, airless room.

Jones had carried a battered briefcase in from the patrol car. He set the black case on the edge of the table, flicked open the locks, and opened the lid. He sorted through the usual mess of papers and folders and pencils until he found a slim black tape recorder. Jones set the recorder on the table between them, and put a legal pad and pen by his elbow.

"Okay," he said. "I know you folks have had a rough day. But walk me through what happened out there at the cabin. We'll need to do in-depth interviews with both of you as the investigation progresses, but for now just sketch out the big picture."

Vince made a show of staring at the tape recorder and clearing his throat. As if he were unaccustomed to talking to cops. He almost smiled when he thought: Hell, I am unaccustomed to talking to cops. In the past, he wouldn't say a word without a lawyer present. But this was a tricky situation. A lawyer would make it look as if he had something to hide. This time, Vince would speak for himself.

Maria still clung to his arm. She scooted even closer, leaned her head against his shoulder as he began to speak.

"It all started last night. Those two boys, their last name's Daggett, and the other one, Roy somebody, tried to rob Shasta Liquors up the road from our cabin.

"It didn't go so well. The one in the duct tape, Junior, tried to stick up those ladies at the store without any bullets in his gun. They apparently broke some bottles over his head before he could get away."

Deputy Kemp said, "Video camera at the store caught the whole thing—"

The lieutenant looked at her sharply and she clammed up. Jones turned to Vince and said, "An unloaded gun?"

"That's what they said. I don't know why. They seemed to have plenty of bullets today."

He paused, waiting to see if Jones had more questions, but the lieutenant just nodded for him to continue.

"They must've seen our lights on because they stopped at the cabin. Forced their way inside and pointed guns at us and ordered us to bandage up Junior. Fortunately, Maria here used to be a nurse."

He reached over and patted her on the forearm. She clutched his arm tighter.

"She did a dandy job of keeping the boy from bleeding to death. Pulled several big pieces of glass out of his scalp."

Deputy Kemp made a face. The lieutenant remained impassive.

"We hoped they'd leave once she helped them, but they stayed all night, keeping us at gunpoint."

Maria nodded against his shoulder. He patted her arm again.

"We figured those boys didn't have any reason to harm us. They just needed a place to hide."

Vince felt Maria shift beside him, but she said nothing. He knew what she was thinking: They headed now into uncharted territory. Everything he'd said so far had been the truth. Now it was time to do some fancy dancing.

"This morning, they decided they wanted a different car. They made me drive them into town to get one. They left the injured one, Junior, at the cabin with Maria and gave him a gun. To make sure I'd cooperate. Told me he would shoot her if I didn't do as I was told."

He paused. Jones squinted at him, his lips clamped together. Vince wasn't sure the lieutenant was buying the story, but it was too late to turn back now.

"While we were gone, Deputy Kemp here came by the house. She noticed blood on the sidewalk, which had been left last night when Junior came stumbling up to the house with his head bleeding."

Jones shot Kemp a look, but the young deputy didn't seem to notice. She was too engrossed in Vince's tale.

"She knocked on the door, and Maria talked to her out on the porch. What the deputy didn't know was that Junior was just inside the door, holding a gun on Maria to make sure she didn't say the wrong thing."

Jones' eyebrows shot up, and again he stared at Kemp, who must've felt it this time. She blushed.

"No way she could've known," Maria said. "He was hiding out of sight. I made up a story, told her Vince had run over a dog with his car and that accounted for the blood. Sorry I lied to you, Deputy Kemp."

A smiled flickered on the deputy's face. "That's okay."

The lieutenant frowned.

"Meanwhile," Vince said, "I'd taken the other two downtown to get a car. They got out of my car to do their dirty business, and I took off."

"You did *what*?"

"Caught them off-guard. They figured an old bird like me would do what he was told."

"You drove away? But they had your wife, holding her at gunpoint. Didn't you think about that?"

"That's *all* I was thinking about," Vince said, and Maria gave his arm a squeeze. "I figured they'd have no use for us once they got a car. No telling what might happen then."

"Why didn't they just take *your* car?" Jones asked.

Vince pursed his lips. "Don't know," he said finally. "Maybe they wanted something with more horsepower."

Vince remembered the little Toyota. No horsepower there.

"When I took off on them," he said quickly, "they probably

just stole whatever they could get. Didn't you say it was a carjacking? They were in a hurry. We were in sort of a race, to see who could get back to the cabin first. Me, to try to get Maria out of trouble. Them, to silence us both."

Jones ran his hands over his face, and rubbed at his eyes. He looked tired. Vince knew exactly how he felt.

"I got there first," he said. "I tried to sneak up on him, but Junior got the jump on me. Then he had Maria *and* me. Holding a pistol on us the whole time. And that's when Deputy Kemp stopped by again."

"*What*?"

Kemp took a sudden interest in the wanted posters on the far wall.

"She'd checked out Maria's story about the dog, called some vets and stuff. She's a sharp cookie, this one."

Vince pointed at the deputy, who blushed furiously at the praise. Jones looked more exasperated than ever.

"We invited her in, and I told her a windy story about how the dog had died and I'd taken him to get buried," Vince said. "Junior was in the kitchen the whole time. I figured that if I tipped her off, there'd be a shootout and somebody would get hurt."

Jones looked from Vince to Kemp and back again, his face flushing and his brows knitted.

"I could tell she was suspicious," Vince said, trying to help Kemp save face, "but she finally left. Little bit later, Maria was in the kitchen with Junior. He got busy watching me, and she got an idea. When he turned back to her, she hit him in the face with a frying pan."

Vince allowed himself a chuckle.

"She really laid him out. We got some duct tape and tied him up before he could come to. We were about to call 911, get some help out there, when the other two drove up in that little blue car."

"Why didn't you call immediately?"

"Well, we were torn." Vince leaned back and stretched out his legs under the table. "Take time to call 911, or defend ourselves? Figured we'd be better off tying Junior up and using his gun. No telling how long it would take the law to get way out there. Turned out, of course, that we probably guessed wrong. It was no time at all before Deputy Kemp was back, right after the shooting started."

Again, Jones glared at the deputy. Apparently, she'd had enough. She looked right back at him, and her chin jutted defiantly. Vince nearly laughed out loud.

Jones said to Vince, "So you just started shooting at them?"

"Not at all. I yelled out the door, told them we had Junior and we had his gun and they'd better back off. Instead, they started shooting at the house."

"And you shot back."

"What else could we do? I winged one of them, the one that later ran off. Clipped his shoulder."

He felt Maria stiffen beside him. She wouldn't like it, him taking the blame for shooting Roy. He talked faster, not letting her interrupt.

"Leon rushed up onto the porch, tried to force his way inside. I hit him in the nose with the gun, and was wrestling around with him when Deputy Kemp here came to our rescue. She rolled up and the wounded one, Roy, shot at her, broke her windshield. She fired back and he ran off into the woods. She made the rest of us lie down on the porch. Leon tried to make a break for it and hit her in the face before she could get the cuffs on him. But she handled him, too."

Kemp's head snapped up. She opened her mouth to fill in the details about Vince saving her from Leon, but he cut her off.

"Yes, sir, she really saved the day."

The deputy shut her mouth. She stared at Vince, and he knew she was calculating how much to tell, whether she could let his version stand. He imagined her weighing the truth against the good he might be doing her career. He slipped her a smile.

"Don't know what we would've done," he added, "if she hadn't gotten there when she did."

Jones coughed. Like he was choking on the story.

Vince decided to wrap it up. Make Jones ask questions to fill in the blanks. These small-town cops would feel happier if they felt they were piecing it together themselves.

"That's about it," he said. "I leave anything out, Maria?"

"No," she said beside him. "That's exactly the way it happened."

Jones straightened in his chair and his eyebrows rose.

"Aren't you leaving some things out?" he said.

Vince cocked an eyebrow at him, not worried. If Jones had bought the story so far, filling a few holes shouldn't be much of a challenge.

"Like what?"

Jones leaned across the table toward him, his eyes fierce and unblinking. "The bank robbery?"

41

Maria nearly yelped in surprise when Lieutenant Jones mentioned the bank. My God, were they onto Vince the whole time? Had they known all along?

Jones' eyes narrowed, and Maria felt heat rising in her cheeks. She sat up straight, pretended to cough, trying to cover. Jones kept his attention on Vince, who, as usual, played it cool.

"Did you say *bank* robbery?" he said.

"A North State Bank branch downtown," Jones said flatly. "Robbed this morning. You telling me you don't know anything about that?"

Vince shook his head. Maria dared a glance at him, saw that his blue eyes were open wide, faking wonderment.

"You think that had something to do with our situation?" he asked the lieutenant.

Jones' brow furrowed. "Can't say. But Redding PD seems to think so. I talked to them on the radio right before we left your cabin. The carjacking happened ten or fifteen minutes after the bank was robbed. And the robbers left a stolen car at the bank. It had a flat tire."

Vince shook his head, as if he couldn't grasp these new facts, as if they were coming too fast at him. Maria knew his mind must be whirring, working things out, probably three moves ahead of the lieutenant.

"You think those boys tried to rob a bank?" he asked.

"Maybe so," Jones said. "Once you ran off and left them, they might've stolen a car and robbed the bank on their way back to you."

"Then they got a flat," Vince offered. "Had to find *another* car to get to the cabin and pick up Junior."

Jones waited, but Vince said nothing more. Finally, the lieutenant said, "Think it could've happened that way?"

"Maybe so," Vince said. "It would explain why it took them so long to get back to our house. I mean, we had time to talk to Deputy Kemp and knock out Junior and tie him up, all before those boys returned. Makes sense if they were busy getting two different cars—"

"Yeah, but there are problems with it," Jones said. "For example, where they'd put the loot?"

"What loot?"

"From the bank robbery." Jones seemed frustrated. "Wasn't in that Toyota. We looked."

Vince shrugged. Maria tried to look puzzled. It wasn't hard. All these facts and suspicions coming at them so fast. She could barely keep up.

"Maybe that other guy, Roy, has the money," Vince said. "The one who ran off."

The lieutenant sat back in his chair, his lower lip pooched out as he considered that.

"Possible," he said. "I'll mention that to the Redding detectives."

Silence fell over the table. Maria sat very still, waiting, praying that Jones wouldn't take the next leap in logic and put Vince at the scene of the bank robbery. Then he turned to her.

"What about you, Mrs. Carson? Anything to add?"

Maria gulped and shook her head. "Seems like that's everything. I can't believe those boys robbed a bank while they were running around town."

"Maybe they didn't do it," Jones said. "But it seems to fit."

"Yes it does," she said. "I just have trouble believing it."

"Why's that?"

"Well," she said, wrapping her hands around Vince's arm again, bracing him for what was to come, "don't think ill of me for saying so, but those boys seemed too, well, too *stupid* to be bank robbers."

Deputy Kemp laughed out loud. So did Vince. Even Jones looked like he was having trouble keeping a smile off his face.

The lieutenant clicked off the tape recorder and got to his feet.

"All right, that'll do it for now," he said. "I need to get on the radio, see how the search for that other one is going. You folks are in for a long afternoon, I'm afraid. Redding police detectives will want to talk to you, and probably the FBI, too. For now, just sit tight. I'll leave Deputy Kemp here with you. If you need anything—coffee, lunch, bathrooms—tell her and she'll see to it."

"Are we in trouble?" Maria asked. "I mean, for shooting at those boys? Do we need a lawyer?"

"Like you were told at the cabin, you're entitled to an attorney if you want one," Jones said. "But I don't think you have anything to worry about. The information will go to the district attorney, just as a matter of course, but I think he'll see it as a case of self-defense."

Maria nodded. Vince patted her arm again. Comforting her, or urging her to keep quiet? She couldn't tell.

Jones turned to Kemp, looking her over.

"You and I will need to talk further," he said. "But first put some ice on that black eye."

"Yes, sir."

"I'll be back in a few minutes."

Jones left the room, leaving the door open behind him. Deputy Kemp stood, too, but she paused, waiting for her boss to get out of earshot. Then she leaned across the table until her face was near theirs.

Keeping her voice low, she said, "You two did real well."

Maria smiled at her, but the deputy was focusing on Vince.

"One problem, though," she said. "Why did you tell the lieutenant that I took down Leon by myself?"

Vince cocked his head to one side. "Thought I'd make you look good. No sense telling him I jumped into the fray. He'd never believe an old man like me could knock out that big bruiser. And I couldn't have, if he hadn't been occupied with you."

"But we'll have to testify—"

"Don't worry about it. It's a little thing. A sin of omission. Better to let you take the credit. I'm probably already in enough trouble without adding another assault to the list."

Kemp grinned and stood up straight. "Don't see how you're in any trouble. You were a real hero today. Both of you."

"Just doing what we could to survive," Vince said. "If you hadn't shown up in the nick of time, we might both be dead by now."

She nodded, seemed to be thinking it over, then said, "I still don't like stretching the truth. We might ought to tell the lieutenant that you helped with Leon."

"Just stick to the way I told it," Vince said. "It's better for you. And you can bet Leon won't mention anything. That guy won't say a word, if he knows what's good for him. Hell, nobody would believe him anyway."

The deputy nodded again, and Maria thought she should change the subject before she analyzed Vince's story further.

"Go get that ice," she said. "Your cheek's really swelling."

"That your medical opinion?" Kemp smiled when Maria nodded. "Okay, then. I'll be right back."

As soon as she was out of the room, Vince leaned over to Maria, kissed her on the cheek. While his lips were near her ear, he said, "No telling who's listening."

She clamped her lips together and gave the slightest of nods.

They couldn't go over Vince's story again. The room might be bugged.

Maria didn't really need a recap. She could easily support Vince's version when it came time for them to question her separately. He'd handled it smartly, sticking just close enough to the truth to make it all plausible. She liked the way he kept playing up that they were the victims here. Just a couple of senior citizens who'd been surprised by real criminals.

She didn't like the idea of lying to the authorities, but she'd do it to keep Vince out of trouble. If the police wanted to blame Leon and Roy for the bank robbery, maybe they'd overlook Vince's role. He and Maria might walk away from all this yet.

It bothered her that Vince told the deputies he was the one who shot Roy. If they decided to charge him with assault or something, she'd have to come forward, say she was the one who actually fired that shot. She still couldn't believe that she'd pulled that trigger, that she'd actually shot a living human being. More troubling still was how easy it had been, given the heat of the moment.

She wondered whether the deputies had found her pistol, the one she'd slid under the sofa. Then she remembered the bank bags, hidden in the pantry. Oh, Lord, she hoped they didn't search in there.

Maria turned to Vince, wanting desperately to ask his thoughts and plans. But she couldn't say a word.

He smiled at her, his blue eyes twinkling, and she realized he was *enjoying* himself, dancing circles around these cops.

"You, sir," she whispered, "are a crazy man."

He winked. "Crazy like a fox."

42

Leon Daggett's broken nose throbbed and his shoulders ached from having his hands cuffed behind him. He hurt all over and he was dead-tired and his clothes were sodden. It was stuffy in the tiny interview room where they'd placed him at the county jail. He huffed the stale air through his mouth, trying to *think* through all the pain.

He and Junior were in deep shit. Roy, that fucker, might've escaped, but Leon was stuck here at the jail with little hope of ever getting out again. Not with Vince and Maria and that woman deputy testifying against him.

He wondered what Vince was telling the cops right now, what lies that old fucker was spinning. He felt sure Vince wouldn't tell them about the bank robbery. That would be digging his own grave.

Without the bank job, what did the cops have on Leon? Stolen car. Assault with a deadly weapon. Assault on a police officer. Some parole violation shit. Hell, that was nothing. He'd do some time, but at least it wouldn't be forever.

Then, he had another thought: Kidnapping. Shit, that's federal. And the cops could make that case against him for holding the Carsons overnight, at gunpoint.

That old couple probably would make him and Roy sound

like real villains. Hell, it wasn't like we hurt 'em. Well, we'd tried, but, shit, I am the one who came away with a broken nose ...

Then he got a flash. Maybe he could get a lawyer to arrange some kind of meeting with Vince. Tell the old man: I won't mention the bank robbery if you refuse to testify to the kidnapping. Make a deal. They could even work something out that would help Leon get a shorter sentence.

He shook his head, which sent a wave of nausea through him as his broken nose jiggled on his face.

No way Vince would play ball with him. The man wouldn't be pushed. Leon and Roy had thought they could force him to play along on the bank robbery, and look how that turned out. Deep fucking shit. He and Junior under arrest, Roy on the run, and Vince still holding the bank loot.

What if he told the cops to search the cabin and Vince's car until they find those bank bags? But that wouldn't help—Vince would tell the cops the bank robbery was all Leon's idea, and the FBI would be right up his ass.

He shifted on the hard chair, trying to flex his arms so some blood would flow into his hands. The cops who put him here said they'd get him a doctor, somebody to check out his broken nose, but they didn't seem to be in any fucking hurry. He'd been waiting in this glorified closet for a long time.

Nothing to do for now but keep silent, wait for the cops to reveal what he was up against, what Vince had told them. They could interrogate Leon all they wanted, and he wouldn't say a goddamn thing. Why make their jobs easier? Let them figure it out on their own.

He just prayed that Junior had enough sense to keep his mouth shut, too.

43

It was hours later before Debra saw Lieutenant Jones again. She hung around the headquarters building, keeping the Carsons company between their interviews with Redding police detectives and a couple of stolid, suited FBI agents right out of Central Casting.

The feds didn't let her listen in, naturally, but they didn't seem to get much satisfaction from their meeting with the old couple. How could they? Vince clearly didn't know anything about the bank robbery. The Redding PD detectives didn't seem to mind that Debra loitered in the background during their talk with the Carsons, but she didn't learn anything else from her eavesdropping. From what snippets she heard, Vince and Maria told the very same story every time.

Debra pressed an ice bag to her face as much as she could stand it through the afternoon, but repeated trips to the mirror in the ladies' room showed that her eye swelled nearly shut and her cheekbone bore a deep bruise the size and color of a plum. Her body was stiff and bruised in places from her tangle with Leon, too, and she kept telling herself it could've been much, much worse.

She probably should've gone home and gone to bed, given her body a chance to recover, but she didn't want to leave the building while the investigation unfolded. The Daggetts were her collar, and she wanted to make sure nobody forgot that.

It was past five o'clock when Jones reappeared at headquarters. Debra ran into him in the hall as she was on her way to fetch Cokes for Vince and Maria. Jones' shoes were muddy and bits of forest litter clung to his clothes.

"Been out on the search?" she asked.

"Yeah, but no luck," he said. "Thought we'd picked up his trail for a while there, but it petered out in those hills. Hell, the brush is so thick up there, we might've walked right past him and never noticed. I pulled in the search team. The sun's starting to go down, and it's already dark in those woods. Don't want our men stumbling around out there in the dark, especially since your perp was armed."

Debra caught the reference to *your* perp, and it made her glad. The lieutenant still giving her credit for breaking the case, despite all the mistakes she'd made. Despite the fact that Roy had gotten away. Despite the fact that she'd acted when she was off-duty.

Jones looked her over, lingering on her swollen face. Looked like he was trying not to grin.

"You have a nice afternoon there with that old couple?"

"A regular little tea party," Debra said dryly.

"PD and FBI interviewed them?"

She nodded. "I heard parts of it. Their story's the same. Just a couple of senior citizens, shooting it out with the bad guys. To tell the truth, I think they enjoyed the whole thing. You get to be their age, you're always on the lookout for a little excitement."

Jones smiled. "Beats the 'Sunset Special' at Denny's."

"Guess so. Anybody getting anything out of Leon and Junior?"

"Not a word," he said. "But we ran them through the computer and found that Leon's wanted on a number of outstanding warrants in the southern part of the state. Grand theft, auto burglary, that kind of stuff. We checked his known associates and turned up a Roy Wade. Looks like he's the one who ran off into the woods."

"He wanted, too?" she asked.

"Not at the moment, but he's done time in the past. Assault, battery, armed robbery, you name it. These boys clearly fall into that category of criminals who never learn from their mistakes."

Junior Daggett had a clean record, Jones said, but he felt certain Pearl and Coral would be able to identify him as the idiot who'd tried to rob them. Assuming the old sisters could stop fighting long enough to point the finger at Junior.

"The carjacking victim, man named Lim, should be able to identify Leon and Roy once he gets out of the hospital," Jones said. "With all that ammunition and the Carsons' testimony, the district attorney's gonna be turning cartwheels."

"What about the bank robbery?" she asked.

A cloud passed over Jones' face. "A separate issue. So far, the feds haven't been able to put Leon and Roy at that bank."

That surprised Debra. After the initial shock of hearing that her perps were part of the robbery, she'd accepted it as gospel. Now, she felt disappointed that they were *just* carjackers and kidnappers.

"There's got to be some connection—"

"The feds processed the surveillance video from the bank," he said. "Got a pretty good image of the robber. He's not Leon or Roy, that much is clear. We don't know who he is."

"What about the getaway car?"

"The one with the flat tire? Cameras caught it on tape, too, but apparently nobody can tell who's inside. It was raining at the time. I hear the feds are trying to enhance the images to get a look at the driver."

"But they don't think it's our guys?"

Jones reached over and rested a hand on her shoulder. "Don't be so antsy. We've got 'em on a bunch of charges. Let somebody else collar the bank robbers."

She felt herself blushing and ducked her head. Looking down, she noticed that Jones' olive-drab pants were muddy and damp from the knees down from searching through underbrush. Reminded her of her morning conversation with Vince—seemed like a week ago now—when she'd observed that he was sitting around the house in wet pants. She should've picked up on the clue at the time. Might've brought the whole thing to a head faster. Of course, it might also have gotten her shot. She reminded herself that Junior had been in the kitchen the whole time, pistol in hand, listening.

Something still wasn't right with that part of Vince's story, but Debra couldn't put her finger on it. Leon and Roy drove him into town at gunpoint, then let him escape? If he stayed in his car the whole time, how did he get so wet?

Knowing that he'd lied to the lieutenant about Leon's capture made her question the rest. Of course, she couldn't voice those doubts to Jones now. She'd gone along with Vince's version and, as such things tend to do, his description of her arrest of Leon Daggett had become the truth as far as anyone would ever know.

Jones strode down the hall toward the break room, and Debra hurried to catch up. He greeted the Carsons, and thanked them for sitting through all the afternoon interrogation.

"So are we free to go now?" Vince asked.

"Yep. We're done with you for now. Probably be more questions tomorrow, as the investigators sort things out."

Vince nodded, then said, "How about your search? Did you find that Roy?"

"Afraid not," the lieutenant said. "It's getting too dark up among those trees to keep looking. We'll try it again in the morning. Maybe get a helicopter up there."

"Roy looked to be in pretty good shape," Vince said. "A weight-lifter type. He might've run for miles."

"He'll turn up. Those kind always do."

"Too dumb to stay out of trouble," Vince agreed.

Maria, beside him, nodded, covering a yawn with her hand.

"Been a long day," Vince said. "We're both kind of beat. Maybe somebody could give us a ride home?"

"Home?" Jones said. "That might not be such a good idea. Roy's still out there somewhere. Maybe you ought to stay in town. With friends? In a motel?"

Vince shook his head. "Better not. I've got things to do at the cabin. I need to nail some plywood over those broken windows."

"I could put a deputy out there to watch the place tonight," Jones said. "Watch for prowlers."

"Human prowlers aren't my concern," Vince said. "It's the raccoons. Leave a window open all night, and they'll tear the kitchen apart, getting at our food."

He and Maria got to their feet, hitching at their clothes and running their hands through their hair, ready to go home.

"I don't know about this," Jones said. "You want police protection out there? We could post a deputy outside the cabin through the night."

"That's not necessary."

"But what if Roy Wade shows up there?"

"Hell, Lieutenant, I'm not worried about that boy. He's probably far away by now. We'll lock up tight. And we'll keep the phone handy."

"No more shootouts?" Debra said.

Vince laughed. "Don't think Maria wants to go through all that again."

"Okay," Jones said. "Maybe I'll have a deputy cruise by the place from time to time tonight."

"Fine," Vince said. "Whatever you think."

He thanked them again for their help, said they'd wait outside for their ride, then he and Maria walked toward the front door of the headquarters building.

Jones watched them go, then turned to Debra. "Got to admire that old man's grit. I hope I'm still that cocky when I get to be his age."

She agreed, thinking: I wish I was that cocky now.

"I know you must be exhausted," he said, "but why don't you go with me back to South Station and start putting together your reports? If you can finish up tonight, you can take off the next couple of days and rest."

Debra opened her mouth to protest, but Jones cut her off. "I need those reports for the DA. Get the ball rolling on the Daggetts."

"Sure, Lieutenant, but I don't need the time off. If I can get a few hours' sleep, I'll be ready for my shift tomorrow night."

"I think it would be better my way." He squinted at her. "We don't need you out on patrol with a black eye anyway. It clashes with your uniform."

44

Maria and Vince kept quiet, holding hands, on the ride home in the back of the police cruiser. The young deputy who drove them saw them inside, took a look around to make sure Roy Wade wasn't hiding out in the cabin, then bid them good-bye.

As soon as she shut the front door behind him, Maria hurried across the living room, straight into Vince's arms. They held each other a long time. She shed a few tears, and he kissed them off her cheeks.

"It's okay, honey," he said. "Everything's fine."

She leaned back and looked up into his face. "Are you sure?"

He smiled. "It will be."

"But the police—"

"It's okay," he insisted. "Tough afternoon, trying to keep our story straight hour after hour, but we pulled it off. You did great."

"I didn't do much at all," she said. "You dreamed it all up and kept them off-balance. When that Lieutenant Jones suddenly mentioned the bank robbery, I thought I'd wet myself."

He pulled her close again, and his hands ran up and down her back, comforting her.

"Didn't take them long to put two and two together," he said. "But, from their questions, I don't think they've got anything to tie those idiots to the holdup. Not yet anyway. Even those FBI types were having trouble with the timeline."

A shudder ran through her and more tears sprang from her eyes. She felt as if she'd been holding them in for twenty-four hours, ever since those bad boys first burst into the cabin, and the dam was broken now.

"Don't cry, hon. The worst is over."

"I don't know. Don't you think they suspect you were involved?"

"They wouldn't have let us come home if they did," he said. "They're still piecing it all together. And nobody thinks a couple of old farts like us could have anything to do with it."

She gave him a squeeze, then leaned back, looking up into his face, blinking at her tears.

"'Old farts?'" she said. "Speak for yourself."

He smiled and ran a hand over her hair. "Time to embrace old age. This silver hair might be all that kept us out of jail."

"The question is: For how long?"

"Yeah, that's been worrying me, too. They'll put it together eventually. But, look, here's the main thing: We're still alive. We're still together. There was a while there when I wasn't sure that's how it would turn out."

"You're right," she said. "We should count our blessings."

"Look around," he said. "Lot of bullet holes in this place. It's kind of a miracle that neither of us caught one."

She nodded, scanning the living room. Glass and blood on the floor. The blazes of raw wood on the walls where bullets had struck.

"The landlord's not going to be happy," he said. "We need to clean up this mess."

She went to get the broom and a dust pan, sensing Vince was just giving her something to do, keeping her busy, softening the emotional wallop of the past twenty-four hours.

When she returned, he was standing in the middle of the living room, his hands on his hips, looking around.

"Something I've wanted to ask you all afternoon," he said, "but I couldn't with all those cops around. What the heck did you do with my other pistol?"

Maria felt her face flush. "It's under the couch."

Vince cocked an eyebrow.

"When the shooting was over, I just didn't want the thing in my hand anymore. And Debra was outside. I figured if I came out holding a gun, she might misunderstand."

"Good call."

"I didn't really mean to hide it. I just sort of slid it across the floor and it went under the couch."

Vince got down on all fours and felt around, finally pulled out the pistol. He creaked back to his feet, dusting off the gun with his hand.

"Do we need that gun tonight?"

"No. But it sure had me curious, wondering where it had gone." He set the gun on the coffee table, then squatted with the dustpan to help her sweep up the broken glass.

"Might be good to have that gun around," she said. "Since Roy's still out there somewhere."

"Don't worry about him," Vince said. "That boy's gone. Those deputies looked all over this country and couldn't find him."

"Still," she said. "That was one mean boy. If he came back here—"

"He won't. He's learned his lesson. He knows better than to mess with us. You might shoot him again."

She felt herself blushing.

"Still can't believe I did that," she muttered.

"My favorite part of the whole ordeal," he said.

When they were done, they went to the kitchen. Maria made a pot of decaf, stifling yawns the whole time.

"You should turn in soon," he said. "But I want to discuss something with you first."

They sat together at the kitchen table. She fingered her turquoise necklace anxiously as he began.

"We're not in the clear yet. Those boys might tell the cops I was involved in the holdup. You've seen how damned dumb they are. You think Junior can stand up to an interrogation?"

Maria shook her head. Junior couldn't stand up to his own brother, much less a bunch of tough cops waving fistfuls of evidence at him.

"There are other things, too. Security photos, the bank tellers who saw me. If the cops get suspicious, I could end up in a line-up."

"But you wore a disguise."

"Yeah, but was it good enough? And there's one more thing—fingerprints. I protected myself against leaving prints in the bank, using your nail polish on my fingertips. But the cops took away my gun before I had a chance to wipe it down. It's bound to have some of my old prints on it. They'll run that gun through a crime lab, just as a matter of course, and they'll find those prints. With the computers they've got these days, it won't be long before they turn up my record."

"That doesn't mean they'll put it together with the bank—"

"They might," he said. "You feel like taking that chance?"

Of course she didn't want to take the chance. But she saw no way to avoid it. She waited silently.

"There's also the matter of my parole violation," he said. "We've known all along that could come back and bite us in the butt. I never should've let that idiot Willis get to me, down in Salinas. If I'd finished out my parole, we wouldn't be in this fix now. We could've told the cops the truth all along."

"Oh, Vince, it's not your fault. You—"

He held up a hand to head her off. "Doesn't matter now. No way to go back and fix it. There's only one safe alternative at this point—we've got to move on."

"We're leaving?" The words caught in her throat, and she blinked back tears.

"I'm sorry, hon, but it's for the best. If we stay here, this is all going to come back on us. At minimum, we'd have to testify in court against those mutts. You think our false identifies would stand up to that kind of scrutiny? And, once they know about my past, even these local yokels will piece it together."

Maria clamped her lips together and nodded. The arguments were overwhelming. He was right. They couldn't stay here.

"What do you want me to do?" she asked.

"Pack up your things. Clothes, photos, paperwork, whatever you can't live without. Don't worry about kitchen stuff or books. Just the things that would be hard to replace. Once you're done, go on to bed and get some sleep. I'll load up the car, and we can leave first thing in the morning."

"And go where?"

"Not sure yet." He smiled at her. "Maybe you should pick a direction, and we'll just drive until we find a spot we like. That worked last time."

She glanced over her shoulder at the front door and the broken windows. "Maybe we should go now, rather than wait for morning. We don't have to pack anything. If the police come back tonight—"

"No. We need to rest. I can't see well enough at night to drive, and you're too tired. Hell, we're both beat. It won't do us any good to take off, if you fall asleep at the wheel and crash the car somewhere.

"Besides, we don't have to worry about the cops tonight. They probably won't even run the fingerprints for days. But they're coming back out here in the morning, to look for Roy and to ask us more questions. It would be best if we're already gone."

Maria nodded and rocked up out of the chair onto her feet. Exhaustion pulled at her like gravity, making it hard to move. She took a deep breath to steady herself and headed for the bedroom to pack.

Sadness followed her, left her blinking back tears. She hated to leave the cabin in the woods and all it had meant to them the past couple of years. But she'd give up the cabin before she'd give up Vince.

She'd do anything to keep him safe.

45

It made Vince heartsick to tell his wife they'd have to leave. She loved the little cabin, loved living out in the quiet forest. They'd built a great life here, until those boys showed up the night before.

He'd puzzled over it all day, trying to find some way to stick it out here, some way to avoid detection. But no matter which way he turned it, he kept seeing cops and lawyers and jail cells in his future. No way for a man to spend his golden years.

He waited at the kitchen table until he could hear Maria moving around in the bedroom, coat hangers screeching on the pole in the closet as she sorted through her clothes. Then he went to the living room and picked up the pistol from the coffee table. He opened the cylinder, saw that only one bullet had been fired. The one that winged that asshole Roy.

Vince carried the gun through the kitchen to the pantry in the corner. He set the gun on a shelf, then moved some canned goods to reach the bank bags. They were right where he left them, which meant the cops probably never searched in here at all. A lucky break. If they hadn't been so busy hunting Roy ...

He unzipped the bags and quickly counted the money inside. A little more than $7,000. He consolidated all the bills in one of the bags, and weighed it in his hand. Not much for all the trouble they'd been through, but enough for a new start in a new place.

He hid the bags again, then went into the kitchen and started a new pot on the coffeemaker. No decaf this time. He'd need caffeine to stay awake all night. He wasn't taking any chances, not with Roy still running loose out there somewhere. Plenty of time to sleep tomorrow. Maria could drive while he snoozed in the passenger seat.

"Vince?" she called from the bedroom. "Are you still planning to board up those windows?"

"Doing that next," he said. "I'll go get some plywood out of the garage."

"Think it's necessary, if we're leaving?"

"I wasn't kidding when I told Jones about the raccoons. They'd find their way in here before morning."

"We don't want that," she said. "We've had enough frights for one day."

He glanced out the nearest window at the dark forest, wondering whether Roy would come back this direction. Probably not. The psycho likely was miles from here. But Vince didn't want to take any chances. He and Maria had survived thus far because he'd been careful to consider every contingency. Not going to change that now.

He took the flashlight from the kitchen drawer to light his way to the garage. And he tucked the pistol into his belt. Just in case.

46

Two hours later, Roy Wade stumbled as he clambered down a steep hillside. His sneakers slipped on the matting of wet leaves and pine needles that made a sponge of the forest floor. He fell on his ass, sliding down the hill, snatching at tree trunks as he tumbled. Bark scraped hide off his hands and arms. Low limbs slapped him in the face.

He stopped suddenly, coming to rest at the bottom of the slope, his left leg splashing into freezing water. He lay still for a moment, heard nothing but his own labored breathing and the burble of running water.

Son of a *bitch*. Wasn't bad enough that he'd spent all day hiding in these woods like a hunted animal. Now he had to fall in the dark. If his bones weren't sheathed in thick muscles, he might've broken something. Then he really would've been screwed. Stuck out here in the middle of nowhere with a broken leg, never to be found, coyotes and buzzards lunching on his carcass.

He dragged himself into a sitting position, pulling his leg and soaked sneaker out of the pool of water. The pool was part of a little creek that gurgled down the ravine. He remembered passing it earlier, when he was fleeing the cops.

Roy had run up and over three of these steep ridges, dodging trees and wrestling his way through a jungle of underbrush. He'd gone more than a mile from the cabin before he went to ground, finding a hidey-hole in a jumble of gray boulders surrounded by a thick grove of manzanitas and brambles. He'd spent the afternoon there, nursing his bloody shoulder and keeping his ears cocked for roving cops, his gun always handy. A few times, the searchers had come so close, he'd held his breath, motionless, listening, but they never found his hiding place in the underbrush. When night finally came, it felt like salvation, but he waited another couple of hours, making sure the cops had called it a day, before he used the cover of darkness to move.

Worst day of his miserable fucking life. Bad enough that the bank robbery had backfired. But Roy hadn't gotten to kill that old man and his wife, a fact that gnawed at him all day. That bitch deputy showing up like that, at exactly the wrong moment. The cops chasing him into the woods. Plus, he'd been shot, which was a new experience for him, one he wouldn't let happen again.

He felt red rage well up within him. He'd kept it tamped down most of the day, too busy being scared. But now he took a few minutes to rest, and the seething anger bubbled to the surface, blinding him, making his head pound.

Fucking Leon and his bright ideas about bank robbery. Fucking Junior and his helpless whining. Fucking rain, which had left the forest dripping and soggy. Most of all, though, that fucking old bank robber, who'd outwitted them at every turn. And his wife, who'd had the nerve to *shoot* Roy. The hell had she been thinking?

The wound still burned on his shoulder. It was just a graze, a notch in the thick muscle above his collarbone. Had stopped bleeding on its own, though the blood had soaked his sweatshirt and one side of his jacket. Roy muttered more curses. He loved that denim jacket, had worn it ever since his last stint in the slammer. Now it had a hole in it, and bloodstains that would never come out.

While the bullet wound was the worst, it wasn't his only pain. His legs ached and his feet felt as if they were swollen to double their normal size inside his soggy sneakers.

Roy hated running, had never believed in roadwork. Better to lift barbells, put some mass on your muscles, rather than run the weight off, sweating along like some dipshit yuppie. But after that deputy showed up at the cabin, Roy had run like he'd never run before. His legs and feet showed the effects of it. He felt stiff all over, too, from squatting all afternoon in that cleft among the boulders, afraid to move or make a sound or even smoke a fucking cigarette for fear that cops would tip to his presence.

Now, he just wanted out of these dank woods. He'd been walking about an hour, trying to retrace his steps, get back to the Carsons' cabin, where he could find the things he needed—some food, cigarettes, a car. Roy had never realized how much he relied on the niceties of so-called "civilization" until he spent hours alone in the forest. What he wouldn't give now to see trustworthy asphalt, nice and flat. Surely he was getting close to the cabin by now. Unless he'd walked in circles the whole time, in which case there was no telling where he might be.

Roy stretched out on the damp ground, put his face down to the pool and drank deeply. Used his scratched-up hands to wash his face and bare-sided head. The water was icy cold, and it refreshed him. Gurgled in his empty stomach, though, reminding him he needed food.

Clumpy clouds still drifted around the sky, but the moon shone through more often now. It was a half-moon, and not much of its feeble light filtered through the thick trees, but Roy's eyes long ago had adjusted to the dark. He thought he could make out a deer trail on the other side of the narrow creek, a way up what should be the last ridge between him and the Carson place.

His shirt had ridden up during his slide down the hillside, and pine needles and dead leaves and God-only-knows-what-else had gotten all over his back. He stripped to the waist and brushed himself off as best he could, then put the bloody shirt and jacket back on. Already cold and damp in these woods, and it would only get colder as the night wore on. He thought about building a fire, but, hell, he'd used his last match shortly after nightfall, braving a cigarette when he couldn't stand the need anymore. A Marlboro sure would be good about now, he thought, then tried to steer his mind away from the craving.

He pulled the revolver out of his belt and ran his hands over it, checking for mud and debris, then wedged the pistol into his hip pocket. Feeling fortified and well-armed, he sucked air into his lungs and set out again.

Roy jumped over the creek and trudged up the hill, pulling himself upward by grasping tree limbs and roots and whatever else he could find in the dark. He reached the top of the ridge and paused, his hands on his knees, catching his breath.

He heard a sound, a long way off. A distant roaring, which he recognized as the jake brake of a big truck. *Vroom-rm-rm-rm*. Probably one of those big-assed logging trucks they'd seen all over this country while traveling the back roads. The noise comforted him. The highway was nearby. He was headed in the right direction.

He picked up the pace as he hiked down the other side of the ridge. At the bottom, he reached level ground. Trees still thicker than shit, but after all the climbing and tumbling he'd done, flat ground felt like a blessing.

Roy followed another meandering game trail, walking briskly now, his hands out in front of him like Frankenstein to ward off tree limbs. He walked for another ten minutes before he spotted the light. A warm yellow glow winking at him as it disappeared behind a tree and then reappeared.

Hot damn. He veered toward the light. Finally, the trees gave way, and he found himself on the perimeter of a clearing.

The Carsons' cabin stood in the center of it, and there was light in the kitchen windows. He peered through the darkness, but he didn't see any cop cars, no sentries posted around the cabin, which meant the old folks were probably inside, all alone.

He pulled the pistol from his pocket and crept closer.

47

Vince was dozing when he heard a noise outside. He snapped awake and sat very still, listening and remembering where he was.

He sat in a straight-backed kitchen chair in the pantry off the kitchen, shelves of food to his left and the washer/dryer to his right. The pantry door stood open, but little light angled inside from the kitchen. At first, he thought the sound might've been Maria, stirring from sleep, and he flushed with anticipated embarrassment. If she caught him in here, sitting up all night among the groceries—

He heard another noise. Definitely outdoors. A snapping twig, the whisper of feet on dead leaves.

Vince hadn't intended to drift off, but he'd been exhausted. A long twenty-four hours of terror, followed by boarding up the front windows and straightening up the cabin and loading up the car for their pre-dawn departure. Sleep hit him the moment he sat still. But he was awake now, and glad he'd made all his preparations.

The front of the house was sealed up tight, plywood nailed over the broken windows, the other windows locked, the bullet-scarred front door dead-bolted. Vince had left the lights off in all of the house, except the kitchen. If that was Roy sneaking around the cabin, Vince wanted him to come in the unlocked back door. He was counting on it.

The pantry was tucked into the corner, beside the back door.

Vince had always thought the design was flawed. When he'd haul groceries in from the car, the open back door would block the way into the pantry, which meant he had to set the bags down in the kitchen, *close* the back door, then move the groceries into the little closet. But he was glad for the arrangement now.

Vince had settled in the windowless pantry after he was sure Maria was sound asleep. It was the one place in the house completely hidden from outside view. And that peculiar way the back door opened meant he would remain out of sight if someone tried to come inside.

Maria should be safe in the bedroom. The dresser still stood against the window, the way Roy had placed it the night before. The bedroom door was shut. And any prowler would have to get past Vince before he could reach her.

He stood up, feeling stiff all over. He looked at the glowing dial of his wristwatch, saw it was nearly 9:30. If that was Roy outside, he'd taken his good sweet time making his way back here.

Vince reached out in the dark, plucked his revolver off the shelf where he'd left it. He hoped he wouldn't have to shoot. If he could just get the drop on—

Another noise. This one very near the back door. Vince wished he had a way to see out there. Maybe this hiding place hadn't been the best idea after all. What if it wasn't Roy at all? What if a sheriff's deputy had come by the cabin to check on things? Worse yet, what if they'd connected Vince to the bank robbery and were out there in force? Bursting out at them, gun in hand, might be the last mistake he'd ever make.

He stood listening, waiting. Heard the back step creak under someone's weight. Heard the doorknob squeak as it slowly turned, the latch giving way.

Vince took a silent step forward, so he was framed in the pantry doorway. When the back door swung open, he'd be behind it, should be able to see whoever entered through the slit between door and log wall. He held his revolver low, his elbow braced against his side, ready.

The back door opened an inch. He held his breath, standing still as a statue. It opened another few inches, paused, then swung the rest of the way. The door blocked the light from the kitchen, cast Vince into shadow.

Roy stepped inside, a pistol in his hand. His clothes were filthy and his face and the naked sides of his head were criss-crossed by scratches and scabs. Blood had dried black on the shoulder of his denim jacket. His head swiveled on his thick neck as he looked all around. His gaze settled on the closed door of the bedroom, and Vince thought the man smiled a little before taking a step toward it. Enjoying himself. Ready to shoot Vince and Maria in their sleep. Rat bastard.

Vince pushed the back door away and leaped forward as it slammed shut. He drove the barrel of his revolver into the side of Roy's meaty neck.

"Drop it, sonny, or you'll be dead before you hit the floor."

Roy froze. Goddamn, the old man had gotten the jump on him *again*. He felt the rage rear up inside him. His vision blurred, the room turning red.

The pistol pressed harder against his neck, felt like it was pinching a nerve. Made his whole shoulder tingle.

Nothing Roy could do but drop his pistol. He unwrapped his thick fingers and let it fall to the floor. He turned his head as far as Vince's gun barrel allowed and glared at the bank robber. Felt a muscle twitching in his jaw.

"You old bas—"

Vince jabbed him in the neck with the gun. Hard.

"Sit down there at the table," Vince said, "while I decide what to do with you."

Roy didn't move.

"Now."

Still, he didn't move. Just kept glaring at Vince, measuring him. They were about the same height, but Roy was twice as wide. If it weren't for that gun, he could snap the old man into pieces like a dried stick.

The bedroom door opened and their heads swiveled at the noise. The wife stood there in a knee-length green nightgown. Her silver hair was mussed and her face was heavy with sleep. One look at the scene in the kitchen woke her right up, though. Her dark eyes widened and her mouth made an "O."

"Go back inside, hon," Vince said tightly. "Close the door."

"What—"

"Right now, Maria."

As the door clicked shut, Roy took advantage of the distraction, ducking away from the pistol and swinging his arm around, crashing into Vince's ribs. The bank robber staggered backward, still holding the pistol, and Roy grabbed his shirt and spun him around, slamming his back into the wall that separated the bedroom from the kitchen.

He got hold of Vince's right wrist and pressed it against the wall. The pistol was pointed at the ceiling, useless. Vince's left arm was loose, however, and he swung a fist, hit Roy on the shoulder, right on the spot where the bullet had done its damage earlier.

Roy roared. Keeping the gun hand pinned to the wall, he swung with his free arm, hitting Vince in the ribs. Once, twice. He could kill the old man this way. Just hitting him in the ribs again and again, until his dried-up organs gave out. Until his heart seized up.

But first he needed to make sure the gun was out of action. He twisted, threw his hip into Vince's gut to pin him against the wall, then used his free hand to reach for the gun. Before he could get hold of it, Vince let the gun drop and it clattered to the floor at their feet.

Fine, Roy thought, I don't need that gun anyway. I'm gonna kill this bastard with my bare hands.

Maria heard the men crash against the wall, and knew things had gone wrong. No way Vince could battle that filthy, vicious boy in a fistfight. Why didn't he shoot him?

She wrung her hands, fear filling her chest. She had to help Vince. But how? She had no weapon. The only phone was in the kitchen. If only—

Another crash against the wall. My God, that boy was killing Vince.

Maria burst out the bedroom door, her nightgown flapping around her bare legs, and found the men right beside her, up against the wall. Roy swung a punch into her husband's chest. Vince's eyes were open, but all the color had left his face. His lip was bloody.

She saw Vince's gun on the floor, near their scrabbling feet. If she could get hold of it, she could put a stop to the fight. She'd shot Roy once. She'd gladly do it again.

Maria dropped to her knees, stretching forward, reaching for the gun. Just as her fingertips touched it, pain rocketed through her scalp as Roy snatched a handful of her silver hair and yanked her up. She stumbled, the pain blinding, but managed to get her feet under her.

She turned her head to the side, trying to see. Roy held her head at arm's length, twisting her hair in his fist. His squinty eyes were bloodshot and feral. His face flushed bright red beneath a cross-hatching of bloody scratches. His lips pulled back from pointy teeth.

Vince slid down the wall and slumped onto the floor, all the wind knocked out of him, his blue eyes glassy. No help there.

Roy yanked at Maria's hair, pulled her closer until their faces were only inches apart. She could feel his hot breath on her face as he looked down at her.

"You want that gun, old woman? Want to shoot me again?"
Maria spoke through clenched teeth. "Nothing I want more."
Roy slapped her across the face. A bright white light blinded
her for a second, then the room reeled. She stumbled, nearly fell as
he turned her hair loose.

"Aw, did that hurt?" he said. "C'mere. Let me give you a hug."
She felt his thick arms go around her, then a crushing pres-
sure as he squeezed and lifted her off the floor. Maria's arms were
pinned tight against her sides. Her feet kicked helplessly. Her face
was even with his, and his foul breath made her stomach roil. Roy
squeezed harder. Felt as if her ribs were giving way.

Her eyes focused on his red face. He was smiling.

Anger rose up within her, sharpening her mind. She knew she
had only seconds before he squeezed the life out of her.

She tried kicking, but he didn't even seem to notice her bare
feet bouncing off his legs. Her vision darkened at the edges, and
she knew her hold on consciousness was going.

Maria lunged forward with her head, her mouth open, and
clamped her teeth on the big man's flat nose. She bit down as hard
as she could, twisting her head to the side, hot blood filling her
mouth, making her gag.

Roy howled. He tried to yank his head backward. She clamped
down all the harder with her teeth, felt cartilage snap. He jerked
away, dropping her to the floor next to Vince.

The big man stumbled backward a couple of steps, his hands
coming up to his face to catch the blood that gushed from his
crushed snout.

Maria gasped, delicious oxygen filling her lungs. She sprawled
on the floor, her head against the wall, Roy's blood dripping from
her chin. She turned her head, trying to look up at him, trying to
see what he'd do next.

Beside her, Vince moved. His arm came up and pointed at
Roy. He had the pistol in his hand.

When he spoke, his voice was a croak. "Be still."

Vince was ready to shoot, but Roy didn't move. His eyes had filled with tears. Blood splashed out of his hands and dribbled onto the floor. His shirt was red with it. Vince's chest felt as if it had exploded. His back ached and his arms shook, but he held the gun steady.

Roy seemed occupied with his pain, with watching the blood dripping from his face. But Vince wasn't taking any chances. He pointed the gun at Roy's lower leg and pulled the trigger.

The gun boomed loud in the kitchen, and Roy's left leg kicked out from under him so suddenly, it was as if it were on strings and somebody yanked on them.

The big man fell hard, landing on his chest, barely twisting his bloody face to the side in time to keep his broken nose from smacking against the floor. Roy pushed against the floor, trying to get up.

Vince slid up the wall and got his feet under him. He leaned over and swung the pistol with all his might, slapping the barrel against Roy's head, just above his ear.

Roy's head snapped to the side, and blood flew from his face, a red arc splattering across the kitchen floor. His eyes rolled around in his head, but he wasn't unconscious.

Vince hit him again, crashing the gun butt against the side of his face, right where his jaw connected to his skull. Something popped inside there. Roy flinched all over, his arms shooting out before him as if he were reaching for something. Consciousness, maybe.

Vince stepped around him, kicked Roy's gun into the living room. He kept his own gun pointed at the fallen man, not quite believing he wouldn't jump up again, try something else. But Roy was out cold.

Maria gagged and coughed, spitting blood on the floor. Vince squatted beside her, every muscle screaming with pain.

"Hon? Are you hurt?"

She looked up at him. Her chin and cheeks were smeared with Roy's blood. Her silver hair was wild, and a clump had been pulled out, the loose strands tangled among the others. She wiped at her mouth with a trembling hand.

"Is he dead?" she asked.

Vince shook his head.

"Too bad."

"Want me to shoot him again?"

She seemed to think it over before saying, "No. But we'd better tie him up before he wakes up."

Vince nodded. "Got any more of that duct tape?"

A wry smile crinkled her face.

"Lots."

48

Deputy Debra Kemp hammered at the computer keyboard, finishing up her report. She wasn't a great typist on her best day, and exhaustion made it worse. She couldn't type a single sentence without backing up and making corrections. She glanced up at the wall clock, saw that it was nearly 10:00 p.m. God, she'd been at it for hours.

Didn't help that she kept getting interrupted. The night shift wanted to hear about her shootout with the carjackers. One deputy after another stopped by her desk, grinning and jawing, before heading out to patrol Shasta County. Debra tried to keep her accounts short and humble. Tried not to boast, Coral and Pearl in the back of her mind. But she'd made a good collar at that cabin, one that would help solidify her reputation in the department, and she couldn't help but be proud. Would've been even better if the perps had turned out to be bank robbers as well, but she shouldn't be greedy.

The timing still seemed fishy, though. Leon and Roy carjacking poor Mr. Lim outside that gas station, only minutes after the bank robbery. Sure, it was raining and they were in a hurry to beat Vince back to the cabin, but why did they take such a chance, stealing Lim's car in such a public way? There must've been plenty of unoccupied cars downtown. For that matter, why did they go all the way downtown to get a car in the first place? They must've passed dozens of parked cars on their way into Redding.

She arched her back to get out the kinks. Lord, she was tired. Bruised and battered and beat. But her mind kept whirring.

She closed her eyes and tried to picture Leon and Roy outside the gas station. Maybe they just panicked once the alarm sounded at the bank, and grabbed the first vehicle they saw. Apparently, you could hear that alarm all over downtown, and they were only four or five blocks away from the bank. Probably sirens nearby, too, as RPD cruisers rushed to the scene. But didn't that just make carjacking riskier? How come these idiots didn't find some other way?

Unless Leon and Roy *were* connected to the bank robbery. In which case, the alarms and sirens would've made them desperate to get the hell out of downtown.

She wondered whether her perps were the ones waiting in the getaway car outside the bank, and whether the FBI photo enhancement would turn them up. That might explain their actions. But if that was the case, who was the third man, the one who actually stuck up the bank? Jones said the feds were certain the robber wasn't Leon or Roy. And it wasn't Junior. According to the Carsons, he'd still been at the cabin, holding them at gunpoint while Debra waltzed in and out, completely unaware—

A thought hit her so hard, it nearly spun her out of her chair. Oh, my God. She leaped up from her desk and hurried toward Jones' inner office.

The lieutenant was coming out the door as she got there, holding an empty coffee cup. He had circles under his bloodshot eyes. Probably needed more caffeine just to keep going. Debra thought she might have something to jolt him awake.

She must've looked a fright because Jones sounded alarmed when he said, "What?"

"That bank robber. Do we have a photo of him from the bank videotapes?"

"Sure. RPD faxed them out all over."

He walked the length of the squadroom, Debra right on his heels, and flipped through papers in a tray until he came up with the photo. He handed her the flimsy image.

She held the black-and-white photo close to her face, studying it, her heart pounding. It wasn't a great reproduction. The robber wore a dark jacket with a hood pulled up over a baseball cap, his eyes in shadow. She could just make out dark, frizzy hair sticking out from beneath the cap. The mustache drew the eye away from the creases on his face.

"You know that guy?" Jones asked.

She handed the picture back to him. "Take a careful look. I think the mustache is fake. And he's wearing a wig."

The lieutenant scrutinized the photo. Clearly didn't get it.

"I think that's Vince Carson," she said.

Jones' eyes went wide. "The old man?"

"Take away the mustache and the wig and he'd look older. Picture him with white hair."

Jones shook his head as he studied the photo.

"Look at his hand where he's holding the gun," she said. "See the veins? That's the hand of an older man. I spent the whole day with Vince Carson. I saw his hands. I think that's him."

He frowned, still not believing it.

"What if Leon and Roy went into town not to get a fresh car, but to rob a bank," she said. "You saw Leon's Trans Am when we towed it in from the Carsons' place. Think a guy like Leon is going to give up a fancy ride like that?"

Jones looked up at her, his high forehead furrowed. Then he looked down at the photo again.

"They take Vince Carson into town with them," she said. "*He* knocks over the bank and then somehow gets away. That's why they were so frantic to get back to that cabin. Not just to save Junior from Vince and Maria. Those punks probably could give a shit about Junior. It was because Vince Carson had left them sitting outside the bank like a couple of morons."

Jones shook his bald head again. "But why would that old man—"

"Maybe they forced him to do it," she said. "Junior was holding Maria hostage. Maybe they wanted more from Vince than a ride into town."

A long pause while Jones thought it over. Debra tried to calm herself, to slow her breathing. She was so excited, she was puffing like a train. Not the best way to persuade the lieutenant.

"I don't think this photo proves it was him," he said. "We'll need something more. And we need to talk to those old folks again."

Debra nodded. "We know where they are, right? Let's go back out to that cabin."

She snatched her jacket off a coat tree in the corner, ready to sprint out the door.

"Hold on," he said. "Did we fingerprint the Carsons today?"

"Not that I saw."

"Shit. How did that get overlooked?"

"Nobody suspected them of anything. We were all thinking of them as victims—"

"He *shot* somebody! He should've been printed."

Debra bit her lower lip. "Wait a minute," she said. "We've got his prints. They're on one of those guns we confiscated at the cabin."

"Right. I'll call the lab."

Jones punched buttons on a desk phone and waited, still staring at the flimsy photo in his hand.

"Krueger?" he said after a moment.

Phil Krueger was an evidence tech who worked the night shift at the crime lab in downtown Redding. He was the only tech on duty overnight, mostly because he was so prickly no one else wanted to work with him. Debra had always thought working solo, among the microscopes and computers and plastic evidence bags, suited Krueger just fine. And it meant he often delivered results faster than would be expected from a nine-to-five crime lab. Fewer distractions in the lonely dark of night.

Jones explained the situation, and asked Krueger if he'd lifted the prints off the guns yet. He looked up at Debra and smiled.

"You run 'em through the computer yet?"

Another pause. Jones rolled his eyes. Debra could imagine Krueger whining and bitching on the other end of the line.

"Do it now," he said.

"The ones from the revolver," Debra said.

"The revolver," Jones repeated into the phone. "We're on our way out to their place right now. We need those results before we get there. By radio."

Jones listened some more, a flush rising in his cheeks.

"Just do it, goddamnit. You got twenty minutes."

He slammed down the phone.

"We'll take my car. Radio for backup on the way."

They hurried out into the crisp fall night.

49

They'd nearly reached the cabin, two other flashing patrol cars roaring behind them, by the time Krueger paged them, sounding as surly over the crackly radio as he did in person.

Debra snatched up the microphone and keyed it and said, "Go ahead, Phil."

"Ran those prints through the computer," Krueger said, "and the machine practically danced off the desk, I got so many hits."

Debra's breath caught in her chest. She glanced over at Jones, who kept his eyes on the road. They were flying along the highway. Krueger made them wait, naturally. Debra could hardly stand it.

Finally, Krueger said, "Ever hear of a guy named Vince Doman?"

"Doman?" Debra's voice sounded funny in her own ears.

"Guy's got repeat convictions for bank robbery going back, like, fifty years. His prints are on that pistol. I checked, and he was last paroled several years ago. Nothing on him since. No arrests, nothing."

"My God," she said to Jones. Into the radio, she said, "Good work, Phil. Thanks."

Debra's hand shook as she hung the microphone back on its dashboard bracket.

"They were in it together," Jones said. "All of them."

"I don't know, Lieutenant. Maybe they coerced him—"

Jones suddenly hit the brakes. They'd come upon the Carsons' driveway before he expected it. The cruiser was nearly past the pine-bordered driveway before he wrestled it to a halt. Brakes shrieked behind them and Debra flinched, thinking: That's what we need, a quarter of the department's fleet wiped out in one chain-reaction accident. Everyone got stopped in time, though, and Jones wheeled his car through the trees to the clearing in front of the cabin.

The other patrol cars pulled in on either side of the lieutenant's car, all headlights pointed at the cabin, illuminating the porch and the boarded-up windows and the honey-colored log walls.

A thick bundle lay on the porch near the bullet-pocked door. A man bound in gray duct tape, lying on his stomach, his bloody face turned toward them.

Debra and Jones got out of the cruiser, and car doors slammed all around them as the other deputies bailed out, guns in hand. Debra followed the lieutenant up the flagstone walkway. As they got closer, she recognized the man on the porch. When she'd last seen him, he'd been sprinting away, blood on his clothes.

"That's Roy," she said.

He had blood all over his face from a busted-up nose. Narrow, mean eyes. His mouth was agape, showing pointy teeth streaked with blood. His arms were pinned behind him, the forearms wrapped together with duct tape from wrist to elbow. More gray tape was wrapped tight around his ankles. One leg of his jeans had been split up to the knee, and bloody gauze encircled his calf, covering another wound.

"Check the house," Jones barked, and deputies hurried up onto the porch, skirting the bound man, and went through the unlocked front door.

Jones radioed for an ambulance, then squatted near the man's head and looked him over. Debra stood behind him, gaping at the man's battered face and muddy clothes.

"Fancy meeting you here," Jones said.

"Fuck you," Roy said, though the words didn't come out too clearly. He seemed to have trouble moving his swollen jaw. His nose looked as if it had been crushed, and blood still dribbled from his nostrils.

"That old couple's got something against noses," Jones said. "That's three for three with broken noses."

"Hurts to get your nose broken," Debra said matter-of-factly.

"No shit," Roy snarled.

"Tends to get your attention," she said. "Makes you behave yourself."

Jones stood up, looked around the porch and at the black woods beyond the glow of the headlights. An owl hooted, far away.

A tubby, gray-haired deputy, Gary Preston, came to the front door, a little out of breath. "Nobody here," he said. "The closets are empty. Blood all over the kitchen."

Jones nodded. "As I expected. They waited for us to leave, then bailed out before we could link the old man to the bank robbery."

Preston had a piece of paper in his hand. He reached over Roy to give it to the lieutenant, who tilted the paper to the light. Debra leaned toward him, trying to see.

"It's addressed to you," Jones said. "'Dear Deputy Kemp. So nice to make your acquaintance today. Thanks again for all your help. Vince and I left a gift for you on the porch.' Signed, 'Maria.'"

"Nice note," Debra said.

"Guess you made a good impression on them."

She pointed at Roy Wade. "Not as big an impression as they made on this guy. I'm thinking he'll never forget Vince and Maria."

Roy grumbled and closed his eyes.

Debra bent over him and said, "You have the right to remain silent ..."

50

Vince awoke shortly after dawn, sunshine on his face, the high-way thrumming beneath him. He sat up straighter in the passenger seat of the Plymouth and blinked his eyes. Pain stabbed his bruised ribs, and he wrapped his arms around them, felt as if he were holding things in place.

"You were snoring," Maria said. She had both hands on the wheel and a smile on her face.

Moving gingerly, he ran his hands over his face, rubbing away the sleep. "I was wiped out. Not as young as I used to be."

"Seems like you did okay to me."

"All that fighting and shooting wore me out," he said. "Dragging sheets of plywood and those boys all around the house. My back'll be hurting for weeks."

"Guess you'd better take it easy then," she said. "Have a nice long rest."

"What about you, hon? You doing all right?"

"Fine."

"You've been driving for hours. And you hardly got any sleep last night."

Maria laughed. "Not like I could sleep with you and Roy crashing around the kitchen. After that, I was wide awake."

Vince reached over and patted her arm.

"I'm glad we went ahead and left," she said. "I can't imagine what it would've been like, staying in the cabin all night with that boy snarling and snapping out on the porch."

"We probably should've waited until first light," he said. "Gotten some sleep. But I had a feeling about those cops. Better to move on out. Want me to drive a while?"

"I'm okay. We should stop soon anyway."

"Where are we?"

"Oregon. Headed toward the coast. We were getting close to Portland, and I figured we'd spent enough time on I-5."

"Good thinking."

Vince looked out the window. Mountains reared up on either side of the narrow highway, evergreens marching up their steep flanks. Birds swooped and wheeled among the treetops. Puffy clouds drifted around a crisp blue sky.

"Pretty country."

"Quiet, too," she said. "I haven't seen another car since I got off the freeway."

Vince looked over at her. "Just the way we like it."

"I was thinking that, too." She kept her eyes on the road, but her face looked relaxed and merry. She's recovering fast, he thought, getting back to her old self.

"Couple of little towns coming up," she said. "I saw the signs. Maybe we ought to stop for breakfast and take a look around."

"Maybe stop by a real estate office? See if there's anything for rent up here?"

"Little soon to be setting up housekeeping, isn't it? We've gone less than 400 miles. Won't the police send word up here, looking for us?"

"Don't worry about that," he said. "I packed those other ID's I had made up before we moved to Redding. They're in the glove compartment."

She smiled. "So what's our name now?"

"Cole. Vincent and Maria Cole."

"I like it. Short, easy to remember."

"That's the idea."

They rode in silence for a few minutes, Vince admiring the verdant landscape and the clouds dancing around the mountains. "Maybe we can find a furnished place," he said. "Vacation home, something like that. Probably be better if we didn't do a lot of shopping for furniture and stuff. At least for a while. Better to stay out of sight until we're sure everything's cooled off behind us."

Maria steered through a curve as the road crested a hilltop. A valley formed a bowl below them, and the sun glinted on the windows of buildings scattered along the highway.

Vince felt full of plans, as if his mind had been busy the whole time he'd slept. His body might be battered all to hell, but there was nothing wrong with his brain.

"We'll need to ditch this car," he said. "But getting a new one shouldn't be a problem. Always some old junkers for sale in small towns. We'll unload it in a different place from where we settle."

Maria mulled that, still smiling. She seemed to have recovered from her disappointment over abandoning their cabin. And he knew she held no great sentiment toward their heap of a car.

"We'll need household stuff, too," she said. "Dishes and pots and pans. I left all mine behind. And groceries."

Vince waited. When she finally glanced over at him, he said, "Better buy some more duct tape, too."

She chuckled. "Never know when you'll need it."

The car zipped down a long straightaway toward the little town.

"Might be a while before we can get my Social Security money and my pension forwarded," she said. "People might be monitoring my account."

"Don't worry about money. Even after a security deposit on a new place, we'll have plenty of cash. I've got $7,000 in a bank bag in the trunk."

Maria's smile vanished. She hesitated, then said, "That's dirty money, Vince."

"The bank's insured. Nobody'll miss it. Besides, I worked hard for that money."

Her mouth tightened into a thin line. "No, Vince. I won't take that money. We have to give it back."

He'd expected something like this.

"How about this," he offered, "we use this cash to get set up. Then, after things have cooled down, we'll send replacement money back to that bank."

"How would we do that?"

"We'll think of a way. Use a fake address, another state. Maybe we'll send it to Deputy Kemp, ask her to deliver it for us."

That brought the merriment back to her dark eyes. "That .might work. You could stand it? Giving back the money?"

He smiled. "Never done it before. Might feel kinda good."

She glanced over at him, then back to the road. "No more from here on out, right? I've thought about it for hours now, and I think I understand why you kept that bank heist kit in the attic. As a backup, right? In case life with me didn't work out?"

"No, hon, I—"

"It doesn't matter, Vince. What's past is past. I'm only interested in the future. You have to promise me: No more robberies. No more crime. No more secrets."

He let her wait a moment, then said, "Only if you promise to stop shooting people and whanging them with skillets."

That made her laugh again. "It's a deal."

Vince felt a twinge of pain in his battered ribs. He leaned his head back against the seat and closed his eyes.

"I was a little worried about you for a while there," she said. "Whether that bank job would give you the itch again, pull you back into a life of crime."

He could tell she was teasing him. He kept his eyes closed, but he could feel himself smiling.

"Not me," he said. "I like retirement. It's so peaceful."